Track the Grizzly Down

A long, bitter feud starts up between Spook and the Reynoldses when the monster grizzly savagely attacks their new cabin. Jed and his son Randy plan to build up a big herd of longhorns, catching wild cattle in the mountains to add to their original herd. They wish to live in peace with the grizzlies, but as Spook moves from one destructive act to another, he leaves them no alternative but to track him down and kill him. The climax of this vividly real, exciting story of life in the Wyoming mountains of the 1840's is a desperate chase, grim and thrilling.

Other Borzoi Books for Young Readers
by Gus Tavo

THE BUFFALO ARE RUNNING

illustrated by E. F. Miller

HUNT THE MOUNTAIN LION

illustrated by Brinton Turkle

TRACK THE GRIZZLY DOWN

by Gus Tavo

illustrated by LESLIE GOLDSTEIN

Alfred A. Knopf : New York

L. C. Catalog card number: 63-9105

THIS IS A BORZOI BOOK
PUBLISHED BY ALFRED A. KNOPF, INC.

FIRST EDITION

For Miriam

Contents

TRACK THE GRIZZLY DOWN

1 TEXAS, MAY, 1877

Folks in Dog Town thought Jed Reynolds was crazy when he came home from buffalo hunting out west and allowed he was moving his family to Wyoming. They said so to his face. "You're a brush popper, Jed Reynolds," they told him, "like your Pa was before you. You pull up and leave the Brasada, and you'll be like a fish out of water."

3

Jed heard them out patiently, jaw set in a stubborn line. "I was born and raised here in South Texas," he told them when they'd had their say. "All I've ever known was the brush. Reckon my roots here go down deeper than even a mesquite's after water. Why, it wasn't till I went out to Wyoming last year that it rightly came clear to me that this whole country wasn't covered with thorny brush. When the huisache and chaparral and mesquite began to peter out and a man on a horse could look clean across the prairie to a herd half a mile away—man alive, that's what I call cow country."

"Cow country," old Jim Collins, proprietor of the General Mercantile, snorted. "You ain't no cowman."

"Not yet I ain't," Jed said stubbornly, "but I aim to be. I'm getting out of the Brasada, Jim. I'm getting out of thorny brush so thick a fellow has to listen for a cow he's tracking, on account he can't see it. No more getting my clothes torn off or my horse and dogs cut up. No more side-stepping rattlesnakes while I'm praying for a clearing to open up where I can spread my loop."

"There's worse things than catching wild longhorns out of the brush," Jim growled.

"You've got a going business here in the store, Jim. Catching cows is just sport for you. But you know well as the rest of us here that cow catching in the Brasada is getting harder every year. Too many brush poppers, and more young'uns growing up to it all the time. Besides, we all know the wild longhorns are thinning out."

"Jed's right," young Tom Jackson spoke up. "Sets a fellow to worrying of nights."

"Look at me," Jed went on. "Thirty-five, and what have I got to show for it? A cabin in a clearing. Sixty acres of thorny brush. Fifty-odd head of longhorns."

"Ain't too bad for a young fellow," Jim grumbled.

"Ain't too bad, but it ain't good," Jed countered. "I've got Molly and the boys to think about. Why do you reckon I signed up with that San Antone outfit last year to hunt buffalo? I was plumb desperate to get me a stake, that's why. You all know it didn't turn out like I'd hoped. But how was our outfit to know that by the time we got out there Wyoming's big buffalo herds would be pretty nigh killed off? Why, the prairies were swarming with buffalo skinners grubbing out a measly living picking up buffalo bones to sell. We couldn't tell the Sioux were going to pick last year to act up, either—keeping out of their way sure put a crimp in us hunters."

"But still you made yourself a stake," young Tom sighed.

"Luck, mostly. I made enough to homestead in a

canyon valley there in the Big Horns, made enough to pay a couple of broke skinners to help me build a cabin. I did it because I want something better'n brush popping for my boys. No, Jim, I'm heading out for Wyoming. With the cash I got for selling my place here, I figure I've got a stake that'll see me through the first winter."

Molly Reynolds knew what a hard time the other brush poppers were giving her husband about moving out. She didn't say much, but went about her packing quietly, a little stoop to her shoulders, picking and choosing among their scanty possessions, giving the old cradle that had slept both boys to young Tom Jackson and his wife, portioning out chairs and tables and bedsteads among the neighbors.

Randy, who was past twelve, had missed his father sorely while he was away, and followed doggedly at his heels now, wherever Jed went. It was Randy who told his mother what old Jim Collins had said down at the General Mercantile.

"Jim said any man was a fool that'd trail his wife and young'uns and fifty-odd head of longhorns all the way from South Texas up to the Big Horn Mountains," the boy told her, brown eyes snapping indignantly.

His mother straightened up from her packing,

brushing absently at the yellow curls clinging damply to her forehead. "What'd your Pa say to that?" she asked him.

Randy pushed his battered old Stetson to the back of his head and hitched up his levis. "Pa reminded Jim I'm nigh thirteen," he said proudly. "Pa said us two men can trail fifty head of cattle without no great trouble, seeing as how we've got the three best leopard ketch dogs in the whole Brasada to help us."

A smile quirked the corners of his mother's mouth. "I can guess how Jim liked that," she said dryly, "with him thinking nothing but a bulldog makes a good ketch dog."

"Anyway, Jim says up in Wyoming folks don't use ketch dogs to hunt wild cows." The boy grinned. "He says there ain't no wild cows hiding out in the brush, like we've got here," he finished with a chuckle.

His mother walked over to the window and gazed out across the clearing. Jed Reynolds had chopped that bare strip out of the brush. Twenty feet beyond the corral she could see the high wall of the Brasada brush, dense, impenetrable—mesquite and prickly pear and huisache and black chaparral, with thorns and spikes and razor-sharp spines that could tear a man's clothes off his body or slash a horse or gouge out a dog's eyes.

"Of course, Jim thinks that," she said over her

shoulder. "That's what your Pa used to think, before he went west to Wyoming. Ever since you were a little tyke, Randy, you've heard folks tell how long-horns used sometimes to stray off from Mexican herds and swim the Rio Grande and hole up in the brush here in the Brasada."

Randy nodded.

"Well, Jim and the rest just naturally think the Brasada's the only place cattle have gone wild and bred up year after year deep in the brush, till now they've got to be hunted down like wild animals."

"I'm sure proud Pa didn't tell our secret, Ma."

"If your Pa'd once breathed there's wild longhorns for the catching up in Wyoming, and in timber instead of thorny brush, half the brush poppers in the Brasada would be heading out there, including Jim Collins."

She turned back from the window just as the door burst open and a little boy stormed into the cabin, yellow curls on end, blue eyes blazing. Three big, spotted dogs cavorted at his heels.

"Hi, Mr. Sam," said Randy, grinning.

"Sammy Reynolds, you get those dogs out of here," their mother ordered. "Nugget! Pard! Polky! Out!"

The dogs retreated. Randy followed them to the door. He stooped and fondled the ears of the big gray. The dog crowded against his legs, brown-and-black-spotted body wriggling ecstatically.

"Out, Pard," the boy said softly. "I'll saddle Pepper after a bit, and we'll have us a run. Go on, now."

He closed the door after the dogs. His little brother was hopping up and down in the middle of the floor. "Ma," he bleated, "Tommy says the Big Horns is plumb full of Injuns. Randy, you got to learn that old Pard to mind me. Ma, Tommy says real scalping Injuns!"

"Stuff and nonsense," his mother said matter-of-factly. "Tommy's just put out because they're not moving too. Your Pa says all the Indians are living on reservations now, since the big showdown General Custer had with the Sioux last year. Don't reckon the government wants any trouble of that kind again. You tell Tommy that Pa's already got our cabin built, all snug and ready for us."

"But don't tell him there's w-i-l-d- c-o-w-s waiting for us, too," Randy spelled, grinning at his mother.

"You quit that spelling!" Mr. Sam yelled furiously. "Ma, you make Randy quit! Him and Pa is always spelling. You just got to learn me how to spell, Ma!"

"Reckon your Ma'll have time aplenty for that, Mr. Sam," a man's voice drawled from the doorway, and Jed Reynolds was there. He stepped into the cabin, a tall, dark-haired man, with wide shoulders and weather-beaten face. He stood grinning down at the little boy. "You and Ma'll be riding in the wagon for three months, Mr. Sam. Ma can sure teach you how to spell in three months."

"I'm going and tell Tommy Ma's going to learn me!" Mr. Sam squealed, and scuttled out the door.

Jed looked smilingly from his wife to Randy. "Three months, God willing, and we'll be in the Big Horns," he said softly. "Just wait till you set your eyes on those mountains, Molly. All over snow on the peaks, glistening in the sunshine. And pine and spruce growing right down to our cabin in Bear Claw Canyon."

"Tell how you found our canyon," Randy begged.

"It was just like I told you," his father began. "By the time our outfit hit Wyoming, the big buffalo herds were nigh killed off. We were hunting down what stragglers were left. One day I was chasing a couple of mangy cows up a strip of prairie between two mountains. They crossed this little river—more like a creek, it was—with the water churning down around big boulders."

He walked over and sat down on a cane-bottomed chair, tilting it back against the wall. Molly sank down on the edge of the bed, her eyes on her husband's face.

"Water wasn't more'n belly-deep on Corker," Jed went on. "I followed the buffalo north up the far bank and through a narrow gap between high cliffs. All of a sudden I rode smack out into a wide canyon valley, with mountains rearing up high on all sides and the little river tumbling down through miles of green grass."

"Don't forget the wild longhorns!" Randy cried.

His father smiled. "Not likely, not since they're the reason I homesteaded in that canyon. Those wild longhorns had been grazing along the river when the buffalo came busting in. Now they were hightailing it for timber. Maybe a hundred of them. It was a sight, with the sun flashing off those long horns."

"Pa, you sure nobody up there knows about Bear Claw Canyon and the wild longhorns?"

"Son, there's hundreds of canyons like ours in the Big Horns. Don't reckon nobody knows them all, except maybe the Sioux and the Crows. Wyoming's thin settled. All I rightly know is what folks in Cheyenne told me. About five years back, Indians stampeded a herd of fifteen hundred Texas long-horns, right after the trail drivers forded them across Powder River. The Indians killed off maybe a couple hundred cows. The rest stampeded for the mountains, and nobody's seen hide nor hair of them since. That's why folks up there call them the vanished longhorns. It was pure luck, me running onto a bunch of them."

"Randy says you and Jim Collins had words down to the store," Molly told her husband.

Jed grinned. "Old Jim was spouting off, like usual. Seems like Jim can't tolerate the notion of anybody doing anything he ain't in on. He takes a powerful dim view of any country where there's grizzlies, like in Wyoming."

Molly smiled faintly. "I'm nigh as bad as Jim," she confessed. "It was the grizzly-claw necklace that Sioux Indian gave you that did it. I get the shivers every time I see it hanging there on the wall. I never saw bear claws like that before, so white, and cruel curved, and longer than a man's fingers."

Jed set his chair down with a thump. "That's exactly why I hung the necklace on the wall, Molly. I want Randy and Mr. Sam to study those claws. I don't want them to forget for one minute what kind of country we're heading into. They've got to learn right now a grizzly's no bear to mess around with. You put claws like that on the front paws of six or eight hundred pounds of meanness and muscle, and you've got a killer brave men are mighty careful not to spook. Randy, fetch me down that necklace."

He took it from Randy and spread it out across his big hand. "Look at it, Molly," he said softly.

She stared with revulsion at the circle of white claws alternating with red beads on a buckskin thong. "They look downright wicked," she said hotly. "It's a heathen notion, making a necklace out of claws."

"Well, I reckon Indians be heathen," Jed said slowly, "but the Indian that killed this grizzly was a brave heathen. This necklace is old, Molly. It'd been handed down from father to son to the Sioux I pulled out of quicksand in Powder River. When that Sioux gave it to me for saving his life, he was giving me the best he had."

"I reckon," she said dubiously.

"Well, he was. Think, Molly, how much spunk it took those old Indians to face up to the mightiest beast in the whole West with nothing more'n an old muzzle-loader or maybe just a bow and arrow and then a hand-to-hand fight to the death with a knife. No wonder an Indian with a necklace of claws off a grizzly he's killed is top man in his tribe."

"I still don't see why you've got to hang the heathen thing out in plain sight," Molly murmured.

"I want our boys to see these claws. Whether we like it or not, we're going to have grizzlies for neighbors. Me and the skinners spotted half a dozen anyway while we were building the cabin. They didn't give us no trouble, and we didn't give them none.

I aim to try to live in peace with them, unless a grizzly comes between me and raising cattle. If one does, I aim to track him down and kill him."

"Golly, but I'd like to put the dogs on a grizzly trail," Randy cried. "I'm fair itching to bag a big grizzly."

Jed got to his feet. "We ain't moving to Wyoming to hunt grizzlies," he said flatly. "We'll have our hands full catching wild longhorns and building up a real herd. Deer and elk you'll have plenty of chance to hunt, for I don't aim to butcher a beef this first winter. But the only bear you'll hunt is black bear, and that only when your Ma needs cooking grease."

Randy reached out and touched the bear-claw necklace with one finger. "Just the same, I aim to kill me a grizzly someday and make my own necklace," he said stubbornly.

Jed rumpled the boy's brown thatch. "That'll be the day you stop being a boy, Randy, and get to be a man."

Randy drew a deep breath. "I just don't see how I can wait two more whole days to get started for Wyoming, Pa."

His father's eyes lighted. "Two more whole days," he echoed softly, "then three long, hard months on the trail. Aw, Molly honey, don't look so glum. It'll be worth it, I promise you. Wyoming'll be worth it."

2 WYOMING, JULY, 1877

The stars had begun to pale in the darkness before dawn. Low in the east the sky was streaked with gray. On the prairie, well away from the covered wagon, shadows of bedded longhorns showed black against the grass. The only sound was the muffled thud of Mesquite's hoofs as she paced her endless circle around the herd.

Randy shifted stiffly in the saddle, glanced over his shoulder toward the streak of gray in the east. He dropped the reins on the black mare's neck and rubbed his gritty face with both hands, fighting back a yawn. He was glad he had insisted on riding herd from midnight to dawn. His father needed rest before starting another long hard day.

Out in the center of the herd a shadow stirred, shifted. Randy reined up, body tensing. Old Stomper was getting up.

The big bull rose to his knees. Massive, outjutting horns gleamed dully in the pale light. All around him the cattle came alive, lurching to their feet, bawling forlornly.

It was lighter now. The boy could make out the gaunt silhouettes of the longhorns, their giant, outspread horns. Their bodies had a hollow, shrunken look. This trail up from Cheyenne had been brutal punishment. Day after day the sun had blazed down. Water holes Jed Reynolds had counted on had turned up dry, bottoms caked and cracked. The cattle had plodded for two days now without water.

Over by the wagon there was a flicker of flame, then fire leaped high. A dog barked. All at once Corker loomed up out of the dusk, and Jed was there.

"How they making out?" he asked softly.

"Not so good, Pa. They never bedded down till about an hour ago, and they're already up."

His father sighed. "That'll mean more danged trouble. We're not more'n three, four hours out from Powder River. Happens the wind shifts around to the east and the cows smell water, we'll have half a hundred stampeding longhorns on our hands."

"But we can hold them with the dogs," Randy protested.

Jed shook his head. "Not out here on open prairie, we can't. This ain't the Brasada. We'll just have to ride with them and pray for the best. You grab some grub now, and swap your saddle to Pepper. And Randy, we'd best lay off the water till we get to Powder River. After Ma made coffee there was just a smidgen left in the barrel. Me and you can do without better'n her and Mr. Sam."

The boy licked raw, cracked lips. "Sure we can," he said sturdily.

"Hurry, then. I want the cows on the trail by sunup."

The dogs crawled out from under the wagon when Randy rode up. He spoke to them softly, then swung to the ground. The brown-and-black-spotted gray reared up, forepaws on Randy's chest. Randy hugged him tight.

"Hold still a minute, Pard, and leave me feel your

paws. Say, the cracks are healing fine. You'll do. Down now, boy. I've got to hurry."

His mother straightened up from the cooking fire as he approached, coffeepot in her hand. Randy picked up a tin plate and bent over the frying pan, forking out side meat from sizzling fat.

"Mr. Sam still asleep?" he asked softly.

"Yes, thank goodness. Don't you want a sip of water, Randy, before you eat?"

"No'm," he lied cheerfully, "coffee'll do fine. How's Mr. Sam making out with his spelling, Ma?"

She glanced over her shoulder at the wagon. "That young'un frights me sometimes," she said in a low voice. "You'd think he'd be proud, spelling words like *cow* and *ox*, but not him. Yesterday he learned *longhorn* and *grizzly*."

Randy grinned. "That's Mr. Sam, all right."

"Sometimes I think answering his questions is harder work than driving the oxen," she sighed. "Randy, what's Pa fretting about? I couldn't get it out of him."

"He's worried once the cows smell water, they'll run all the way to Powder River," he said around a mouthful of bread and meat. "Gaunted like they be, they might drop dead running under a hot sun. Pa sure doesn't want to lose any cows this close to the homestead."

She sighed. "We've been on the trail so long it doesn't seem like we'll ever get to the Big Horns," she said wistfully.

"Don't you fret, Ma. Pa says once we're across Powder River, the worst'll be over."

She put her arm around him and hugged him to her. "You've been a real comfort this whole trip, Randy. Your Pa says so, too. Soon as you finish eating, you best yoke up Pablo and Pancho. And hitch Poca to the tail gate with Mesquite, will you? I don't want Mr. Sam yowling to ride his mare today."

"Sure, Ma, I'll take care of them."

"Pa wants I should trail the herd till we're over Powder River," she sighed. "I do dread the day. The dust will be fierce."

The eastern sky was ablaze with gold and crimson by the time they had the longhorns started up the trail. Jed was riding point close beside the lead steer. Behind, the herd was strung out for three hundred yards.

Randy rode halfway back on the west side, the three leopard dogs trotting behind Pepper. The cattle held to a steady walk, heads swinging. Dust rolled up from under their hoofs. Randy pulled his bandanna up over his nose.

The sun came up, a flaming ball in the east. The

prairie was flooded with yellow light. Randy stood up in his stirrups and scanned the wide plain. Nothing broke its rolling surface but clumps of grayed sagebrush. He settled back with a sigh. The day was going to be a scorcher.

Mile after mile fell behind them. Dust hung so thick that Randy could barely make out the outline of the covered wagon trailing far in the rear. The pace of the cattle had slowed. They stumbled blindly along the rutted trail, bawling pitifully, big heads drooping lower and lower under the weight of ponderous horns.

The morning dragged on. Randy slumped in the saddle, head tucked against the dust. All at once he heard his father give a shout. The boy jerked up. The cattle were picking up speed. Their heads were high. They were bawling excitedly.

The boy spurred Pepper into a lope up the line. The dogs raced along beside the stallion. They were almost to Jed when the lead steer broke into a trot. In a moment the whole strung-out line was trotting, wide horns bobbing.

"They've smelled water," Jed shouted as Randy rode up. "They'll make a break for it now."

At that instant the lead steer shot forward, passed Jed, streaked away up the trail at a gallop. Jed sent Corker racing after the runaway. Pepper strained against the bit, whinnying. Randy held him down, heart pounding. His father was riding low on Corker's neck, arm rising and falling as he flailed the sorrel with his lariat. Slowly Corker pulled up on the lead steer. Dust rolled back, half blotting him from Randy's view.

Suddenly from behind came the wild barking of dogs, the pound of hoofs. Randy jerked Pepper around. The herd was running. They had broken out of trail line, had bunched into a solid front, crowding against one another, fighting their way ahead. Without warning a small bunch broke away, angled out to bypass Pepper. Barking wildly, the dogs raced to head them off.

Randy jabbed Pepper with his spurs. The roan stallion lunged after the dogs. Randy risked one quick look up the trail. Corker was crowding the lead steer into a turn, was—suddenly Randy's breath caught in his throat. Corker had stumbled, had catapulted Jed Reynolds straight into the path of the onrushing herd.

Randy yanked Pepper around. His father lay where he had fallen. Corker had recovered and was galloping away, stirrups flopping.

"Pard!" Randy screamed. "Nugget! Polky! Catch the line! Catch the line!"

Over the pound of hoofs, the dogs heard. They

whirled, streaked after the runaway cows. They passed the stampede, cut across in front, straight for the center of the line. The cows in the middle faltered, dodged sideways. The dogs launched into the air. There was a maddened bellow as a dog's teeth closed on a cow's nose. The cow flipped over, legs pawing air, then another and another. Panicked, the cattle crowded to left and right, sweeping past well out to the sides of the fallen man.

Randy spurred Pepper into a run. He could see his father stirring. He reined Pepper back on his haunches beside the prone figure and flung himself to the ground. "Pa," he choked, dropping to his knees. "Pa, you hurt bad?"

Jed pushed himself up on his arms, shaking his head groggily. "Wind knocked out of me," he gasped. "What about Corker? Did he break a leg when he stepped into that hole?"

"Corker's all right. He's over there grazing just like nothing happened."

The three spotted dogs came crowding up, tails beating. Jed sat up and rubbed their heads. "Good dogs," he said unsteadily. "You didn't let me down."

"You want I should fetch Corker?" Randy asked.

"Do. How far back is the wagon, Randy?"

Randy got up, shading his eyes with his hand. "Nigh onto a quarter of a mile—" he broke off, squinting against the glare of the sun. "There's too much dust rolling, Pa. The oxen are running!"

Jed got on his knees, struggled to his feet. He took one look. "Nugget! Polky! Pard!" he shouted, pointing. "Go get them!"

The dogs took off in a dead run, bunched close.

"Randy, ride for the wagon! Get your rope around Pancho's horns! I'll catch up!" Jed turned, staggered across the grass toward his horse.

Randy hit the saddle. He brought his lariat down across Pepper's rump. The roan lunged forward, stretching out in a run, belly low to the ground. Hot wind tore at the boy's face. Far down the trail dust puffs followed the racing dogs. Beyond, Randy could make out the wagon, careening from side to side.

The dogs reached the stampeding oxen. They slid to a stop, turned, and raced alongside under Pancho's horns, crowding him, jumping, forcing him over against Pablo. Slowly the oxen gave way. They swerved off the trail, swung out to the right in a wide arc.

Almost to the wagon, Randy swung Pepper sharp to the left and cut straight across the path of the oxen. The wagon careened past the roan's tail. Randy brought Pepper around behind the wagon and spurred up alongside.

The dogs had the oxen down to a fast, lurching

trot. Randy dropped the reins on Pepper's neck. He twirled his rope, building a loop. The rope snaked out, dropped around Pancho's horns. A moment later, a noose settled over Pablo's horns.

They pulled the bawling, fighting oxen to a halt. Out of the corner of his eye Randy could see his mother, foot braced against wagon brake, body strained back against the reins.

"Molly!" Jed shouted. "Molly, girl, you all right?"

She slumped down then, face drained white. "I— I reckon I am," she panted.

"Where's Mr. Sam?" Jed asked.

At that moment Mr. Sam came up off the floor of the wagon, outsized Stetson resting on snub nose. He shoved the hat up with both hands. "Well, I ain't all right!" he roared. "I'm shook to pieces, that's what I am! Where's Poca? Where's my horse?"

"Poca's all right,'" Randy said unsteadily. "Still hitched to the tail gate, her and Mesquite."

Molly straightened up, tucking loosened hair into its knot. "Where are the cows, Jed?" she asked.

"Belly-deep in Powder River by now," he said grimly. "When they smelled water, they got away from us. No use chasing after them now. Any of them drop in this heat, we couldn't do nothing. Me and Randy'll keep our ropes on the oxen and ride along with you to the river."

3 UNEXPECTED NEIGHBORS

They pushed on, holding the thirsty oxen to a jogging walk. The noonday sun blazed down. The prairie gave way to broken sagebrush slopes and rocky gulches.

It was Randy who first spotted the dark blue line on the horizon to the northwest. He wiped his sweaty face with his sleeve, squinting against the sun. "Pa," he said worriedly, pointing: "those dark clouds up there—"

Jed took one look and gave a glad shout. "It's the Big Horns! Powder River'll be over that high ridge up ahead. We've made it, Molly! We've made it!"

They saw the tips of cottonwoods first, then as they topped out over the ridge, they saw the gray trunks, the heavy green foliage. Beyond the trees was the glare of sunlight on water.

"I see Powder River first!" Mr. Sam squealed.

The oxen went over the ridge and down the long slope toward the muddy yellow river at a jarring trot.

"A mile wide and an inch deep," Randy muttered under his breath. He gazed hungrily at the huge cottonwoods that grew in clumps along the low bank. Real shade trees.

"What'd I tell you about the cows!" Jed growled. "Look at them!"

The longhorns were standing out in shallow water, tails switching placidly.

Randy stood up in his stirrups and started counting. "Fifty-one, fifty-two, fifty-three, fifty-four," he finished. "We never lost one, Pa."

They halted Pancho and Pablo at the edge of the water. Jed and Randy unyoked the oxen while Mr.

Sam ran around to the back of the wagon and untied Poca and Mesquite.

"Hobble the horses as soon as they've watered," Jed told Randy. "Then you and Mr. Sam take the pails up the bank above the stock and fill them. We'll have to settle the water before we can drink it."

Mr. Sam hitched up his levis and sidled over to his father. "Reckon I'll ride Poca from here on,'" he volunteered offhandedly, cutting his eyes up at Jed. "Figure you and Randy'll be needing another hand fording the cows across Powder River."

Jed swatted the little fellow on the seat. "You'll ride Poca when I tell you," he declared, grinning, "and that won't be this side our homestead. Don't you stick out that lip at me, young man. You go help your brother. Scat."

Molly was standing quietly beside the wagon, her eyes on the distant mountains. Jed walked over to her. "Just think," she murmured, "I can ride with my eyes on the Big Horns all the rest of the way."

So that the cattle might graze, they camped there under the cottonwoods. They turned in at dusk and were up while it was still dark. They forded Powder River at sunup. All that day they pushed the cattle hard. At sundown, they made a dry camp. They were too keyed up to rest. They could not stop gazing at the mountains.

At noon next day they reached Crazy Woman Creek. Almost as wide as Powder River, the creek was no more than hub-deep on the wagon. Jed and Randy took the cows across first. Then Jed rode back and drove the wagon over. They pitched camp on the far side, grazing the herd.

Before sunup next morning, they were on the trail. By noon they were into the Big Horns, following a narrow strip of prairie between spruce-and-pine-covered mountains. On both sides of the trail bleached bones lay scattered in the grass, buffalo bones, with here and there a great skull chalky white in the sunlight.

Randy held Pepper well back along the strung-out line. The boy rode gazing up at the timbered mountains, tilting his head back as he studied the jagged granite peaks that seemed to lean out over the prairie. His heart beat fast.

For a couple of miles they pushed slowly forward between the walls of the mountains. Randy kept glancing at a snow-capped granite peak straight ahead. "Looks like what Pa told us about Mount Baldy," he muttered aloud, "and if it is, our river flows along right at the foot. I'm going up and ask him."

He touched Pepper with his spurs, sending him loping up along the line. He was almost up with his father when he spotted the smoke ahead, a thin gray spiral drifting up out of a stand of spruce.

"Pa," the boy called excitedly, "you see that smoke up ahead?"

"I've been studying it," his father told him.

"Reckon somebody's camped in among the spruce?"

"That's smoke out of a chimney, or I'll eat my hat," Jed replied. "Somebody's built a cabin there at the head of the valley since I've been gone."

"Is that good?"

His father took off his Stetson and scratched his head. "Depends on what kind of folks they be," he said cautiously. "If they're the wrong kind, they're too close to our homestead to suit me."

"Look, Pa, horses coming."

"Well, I reckon we'll pretty soon know," Jed muttered.

The horses were moving out fast ahead of a trail of dust. "A bay and a buckskin," Randy announced.

Jed nodded. "Why, looks like a couple of young'uns," he exclaimed. "And the one on the bay mare is a little girl."

He was right. Randy could see her, riding astride like a boy, long red hair streaming out in the wind. A boy was riding the buckskin, a boy just about his size.

The riders reined their horses to a walk as they neared the cattle, swinging well out to one side, approaching Jed and Randy at a walk.

Jed grunted his approval. "They know better'n to spook the cows," he said out of the corner of his mouth. He swung Corker out to meet them. Randy followed.

The boy was short and stocky, with cropped sandy hair showing under his Stetson. He had a wide grin. Brown eyes sparkled with excitement.

"You Jed Reynolds, sir?" he called out.

"That I am," Jed said in surprise.

"They told Pa down to the land office you'd homesteaded in the canyon up beyond our place," the boy told him. "We're sure proud you've got here. I'm Hal Martin, and this is my sister Susie."

"Pa says we're to bid you folks welcome," the red-headed girl smiled shyly. "Mama put dinner on the minute we spied you heading up the valley."

"That's right neighborly," Jed acknowledged. "I don't mind saying I was some surprised to see we had close neighbors. This is my son Randy. The wife and little Sam are riding back in the wagon."

"I'll ride on back and speak to Mrs. Reynolds," Susie told them, reining her mare around.

Hal swung his buckskin into line beside Corker and Pepper. "Your cows are packing plenty tallow," he said admiringly. "Time we trailed our herd up from Kansas, they were plumb gaunted out."

"Well, we've grazed ours slow up from Powder River," Jed told him. "So you folks are from Kansas, are you?"

"Yes, sir. We had a pretty good ranch down there, but the droughts licked us. Then last year Mama's brother moved out here and built a trading post in the settlement. That's Buffalo—it's thirty miles southeast from here."

"I've been to Buffalo," Jed nodded. "Bought my supplies there, off a fellow called Jim Jones."

"That's my Uncle Jim. He said he knew you. He was the one who talked Pa into homesteading out here. Pa's sorry now—folks live closer back in Kansas. Besides, the bears and the cougars around here keep him in a fret."

"Grizzlies been any bother?" Jed asked.

"Not yet, but we've spotted three or four. They sure were big. Uncle Jim told Pa you're a hunter, besides being a cowman. That relieved Pa a lot. He figures maybe him and you can sort of help each other out. Like trailing your cows down to Buffalo together, when it's time to sell."

"Neighbors living as far from the settlement as we do've just naturally got to stick together," Jed agreed. "Say, you folks sure have your place fixed up nice."

They were near enough to see the Martin cabin. Built of unpeeled logs with a steep roof of cedar shakes, it nestled among tall spruce on the bank of a mountain brook.

"Where you grazing your herd?" Jed asked.

"Up there on the slope left of the cabin."

"Where—oh, I see them. Say, you must have better'n a couple hundred head."

"Yes, sir, closer to three hundred. You want to turn your cows out on the grass here? Me and Randy can round them up easy when you're ready to push on."

"Might as well." Jed swung Corker off the trail. The lead steer followed. The long line broke up and moved out onto the grass.

As the cows moved off, Molly drove the wagon up to where Jed and the boys waited. Susie Martin rode alongside. Randy grinned. Susie had Mr. Sam in the saddle before her.

"Whoa!" Molly shouted. "Pancho! Pablo! Whoa!"

The wagon creaked to a stop. Molly leaned out. "Jed, Susie says her folks are expecting us to dinner."

Jed rode over beside the wagon, followed by the boys. "That's right. Molly, make the acquaintance of

Hal. This is the missus, Hal, and that young squirt there with Susie is Mr. Sam."

"Howdy do, ma'am," said Hal, with a friendly grin. "Hi, Mr. Sam."

"We're proud to know you," Molly told him. Mr. Sam grinned, ducking his head.

"Why don't you drive on up to the foot of the cabin slope?" Jed suggested.

They started down the trail. As they rode along, Randy and Hal sized each other up out of the corner of their eyes.

All at once a rabbit popped out from under a clump of sage and bounded off across the prairie. From behind the wagon a dog barked. Hal swung around.

"Say, you've got a pack of dogs!" he exclaimed.

Randy grinned. "Best ketch dogs in Texas."

"Ketch dogs?" Hal asked. "What—look, here come Pa and Mama."

A short, stocky man was hurrying down the slope to meet them. At his heels trotted a plump little woman, apron strings fluttering. Molly pulled the oxen to a halt, and Jed helped her to the ground.

"I never was gladder to see anybody," their new neighbor called, advancing with outstretched hand. "You're Jed Reynolds, I know, and this is your missus. I reckon Hal and Susie were proud to see your boys. I'm Henry Martin, and this is the wife, Sarah."

They shook hands all around. "Dinner's nigh ready," said Sarah Martin, beaming at Molly. "My, but it's good to know another woman's going to live close by. And I reckon Henry'll sleep better nights now your man's here, and him a hunter."

"I never hoped to have a close neighbor," Molly told her shyly, brushing at her long calico skirt. "I'm shamed we're so dusty from the trail."

"Lands, you ought to have seen us when we got here, and we'd only come from Kansas. Anyways, I put a kettle of water on the crane the minute we spied you coming. I knew you'd crave to fresh up. I feel like apologizing for the dinner. There's only a haunch of venison and beans and stewed peaches. Though I did make fresh light bread today."

"It sounds wonderful."

The two women turned toward the cabin. Henry Martin glanced curiously at the dogs cavorting around the youngsters.

"What breed of dogs you got there?" he asked.

"Leopard dogs," Jed told him. "Ketch dogs."

"Come again?"

"We call them ketch dogs down in Texas. Rightly they're c-a-t-c-h dogs, raised to catch wild cows out of brush."

"Called leopard on account of their spots, eh?"

"That's right. The big dun with the yellow spots is Nugget. The gray with brown and black spots, that's Randy's dog Pard. Mr. Sam claims Polky, the white with gray spots."

"How come they're all blind in one eye?"

Mr. Sam opened his mouth for the first time. "They ain't blind, neither!" he blazed.

"That's what's called a milky eye," Jed explained. "Some folks call it a glassy eye. Most leopard dogs've got one. See as good out of it as out of their clear eye."

"Hmm. They any good trailing bear?"

"Bear, cougar, anything you put them on. I ain't ever put them on a grizzly track, but they could do it."

"It's grizzlies what's keeping me laying awake nights," Henry said soberly. "This territory's plumb infested with grizzlies. You'll never know how proud I was to see your outfit coming up the valley. This country's too wild for a lone man and his family."

"I sort of thought it was peaceful like, while I was building our cabin."

"But there again, you're a hunter. Me, I'm nothing but a cowman. Oh, I'm fair good at doctoring, cows or people, but that's about all."

"Reckon I'm just as proud to hear that as you

were that I'm a hunter," Jed told him.

"Between us, we ought to make out all right," Henry said, grinning. "You sure built a nice cabin, Jed. We rode over one Sunday, back in June. Went inside. Figured you wouldn't mind, seeing as you'd just laid a bar across the door."

"You were welcome, Henry. Were things all right?"

"Right as rain. Couldn't help thinking how smart you'd been, laying all them staples in before you came up the trail from Texas."

Jed grinned. "Still had cash in my pocket after I'd paid off the two skinners that'd helped build our cabin. Borrowed a wagon off one of them and hauled the staples up from Buffalo. Figured it'd save me having to make a trip to the settlement before snow flies."

"When did you build the cabin, Jed?"

"Finished it the last of August. Got out just before the snow. I hit Texas the first of November. Sold my place there during the winter and pulled out in May."

"You men come along in," Sarah Martin called from the cabin door. "You can talk your fill at dinner."

Henry and Jed started up the slope to the cabin. The youngsters lingered at the wagon.

"Aren't those bear traps piled up there alongside the cabin, Hal?" Randy asked.

"Sure are. Pa aims to set them if bears start pestering us."

"Randy, what's that you got around your neck under your kerchief?" Susie asked.

"Susie!" her brother thundered. "Don't mind her, Randy. She's only nine, and besides, she's a girl.'"

Randy grinned. "It's a grizzly-claw necklace," he told Susie. "Last summer when Pa was buffalo hunting out here, he saved a Sioux Injun from quicksand down in Powder River. The Injun gave him the necklace."

"Golly," Hal said. "Let's see it, Randy."

Randy untied his bandana and lifted the necklace off over his head, holding it out.

Susie's eyes got big and round. "Gee!" she gulped.

Hal touched the long curved claws. "Gee whillykins, ain't they something!" he breathed.

Randy stuck his finger under a claw and wiggled it at Susie. She jumped back with a shriek. "Randy, don't!"

"Do it at me, Randy," Mr. Sam squealed, hopping up and down. "Wiggle it at me."

"You ever do much hunting?" Hal asked eagerly. "Maybe you and me can bag us a grizzly."

Randy pointed to the carbine in the saddle boot on

Pepper. "I've done right smart, but Pa says no grizzly hunting for us. Pa aims to live peaceable with the grizzlies." He put the necklace back on. "We'll get plenty hunting, Hal. Pa's depending on me to keep us in meat."

"You mean he's going to leave you do the hunting?"

Randy pushed back his shoulders and gave his levis a hitch. "Sure. I kept me and Ma and Mr. Sam in meat the whole time Pa was out here in Wyoming last year."

"Golly!"

"I got me a rifle in the wagon," Mr. Sam burst out. "I ain't never shot nothing but a pesky old skunk, but next year when I'm six, I'm going hunting. I aim to get me a bear cub for a pet, I do. You want to see my rifle, Hal?"

Hal grinned down at the eager little fellow. "After dinner, Mr. Sam. We best get on up to the cabin now, or else Mama'll start hollering for us."

4 THE RAVAGED CABIN

After dinner Randy and Hal rode out with the dogs
and rounded up the cattle. Jed and Molly and Mr.
Sam were waiting with the Martins at the wagon
when the boys brought the bawling longhorns in.

"I'll lead out," Jed told Randy. "Ma'll follow
me with the wagon. Get the cows strung out, then
drop back and ride drag."

"Yes, sir."

"Oh, my lands, I near forgot!" Sarah Martin cried. "Wait a minute before you get going."

She trotted up to the cabin. In a moment she came hurrying back, a big willow basket in her hands. She handed it up to Molly in the wagon. "So's you won't have to start cooking right off," she panted.

Molly peeped under the white cloth which covered the basket. "Venison and light bread," she exclaimed. "You shouldn't have, Sarah."

"Sure will beat the jerked elk I left in the cabin," Jed grinned. "I'd figured we'd have to do on that and sowbelly till Randy fetched in fresh meat."

With the Martins waving good-by they started out, Jed riding beside the wagon. Randy and the dogs whipped the cows into line. They trailed the wagon for half a mile down a gentle slope to a narrow river. The cows followed the wagon docilely into the shallow, churning current. On the far bank Jed swung left, leading the way slowly in and around scattered clumps of spruce and pine, skirting the mossy boulders which dotted the slope of Mt. Baldy.

Randy's heart beat fast. He knew from what his father had said that they were close now to their canyon. Ahead he could see a narrow gap between high rocky walls. The wagon entered the gap and vanished around a sharp turn. The cows followed, bawling, crowding, wide horns clicking.

Boy and dogs trailed the cows through the winding passage. The farther they went, the more the rocky walls seemed to close in overhead. Then suddenly they eased around a sharp bend. Before them a wide canyon valley opened out.

The boy caught his breath. Bear Claw Canyon stretched east and west, with rocky cliffs and timbered mountain slopes walling it in. A narrow stream, its low banks bordered with willows and cottonwoods, churned down through the wide meadow. Across on the north side of the canyon, a hundred feet beyond the stream, the cabin nestled in a half circle of giant silver spruce.

Randy let out his breath in a long sigh. He whistled to the dogs, then touched Pepper into a lope up along the line of cows. The wagon had pulled up just short of the stream. Already the cows were scattering out into the grass.

Randy reined up beside his father. Jed was holding Corker with a tight rein. His eyes were on his wife's glowing face. He turned slowly and smiled at Randy.

"Well, Son?" he asked expectantly.

Randy tried to swallow the lump in his throat. He wanted to tell his father how he felt. He wanted words for the beauty of the canyon. "It's—" he began, then hesitated. "It's sure something!" he finished in a burst, and his words were enough.

They forded the stream and started up the slope toward the cabin. Randy rode watching his mother's face. Her eyes were shining. The boy knew why. His father had built their cabin without haste, carefully matching the unpeeled logs, calking the two big windows neatly, using white rock for the tall chimney at each end. A split-log step led up to a wide porch which ran the length of the cabin. Its roof was supported by peeled cedar posts. Nailed squarely over the step was a pair of huge elk antlers.

Molly pulled up before the cabin. Jed and Randy dismounted and helped her to the ground. Mr. Sam clambered down over the wheel. "Golly, look at them big deer antlers!" the little fellow squealed.

"Those are off an elk bull," his father corrected. "I shot him one evening when he came down to the river. Wait till you set your teeth in the elk meat I jerked."

"Aren't you going to unbar our door?" Molly asked.

Jed led the way up onto the porch. He lifted the heavy bar and swung the door wide. "You first, Molly."

She stepped across the threshold, Randy and Mr.

Sam at her heels. Suddenly she screamed. With a stifled cry, Jed leaped through the doorway. He brought up short. His mouth sagged open. The cabin was a shambles. Jed stared unbelievingly at the big rectangular splash of sunlight on the floor.

"The roof!" Molly wailed. "Look at the roof!"

Dazedly Jed's eyes followed slanting sun rays up to a wide, jagged hole in the roof.

"The back door's tore clean off!" Mr. Sam bellowed.

The dogs had crowded past them. They were nosing over the floor with low growls, hackles bristling. Jed followed them slowly toward the cooking fireplace at the east end of the cabin. Dried beans crunched under his boots. All at once he halted, stared incredulously up at the rafters.

"The jerked elk! It was hanging up there! It's gone!"

He swung back toward the fireplace. "And all the staples I laid in . . ." his voice trailed off.

Molly and the boys went to him. The shelves Jed had built from floor to ceiling on both sides of the cooking hearth had been ripped from the wall and shredded into jagged splinters. Tattered strips of sacking lay scattered over caked patches of flour on the floor. The hand-hewn floor boards were scarred with long parallel gouges.

Stooping, Jed picked up an empty syrup bucket, the lid twisted off, sides perforated with small holes. Dribbles of syrup had dried brown and hard on the metal.

Mr. Sam tugged at his father's sleeves. He held up a small can. "Something's went and punched holes all over and drank the milk," he complained.

The syrup bucket dropped to the floor with a clatter. Jed's face was tight. "Not just something." His voice grated. "It was a bear, and a big one, judging by that hole in the roof."

Randy shivered. He glanced at the dogs. They had the bear smell. They were snuffling over the litter on the floor, tails beating. By the jagged hole where the back door had been splintered off its hinges, Pard was working over the flour-coated floor. Randy walked over to him. The dog looked up and whined deep in his throat.

"What is—" Randy began, then broke off. "Pa!" he called. "Here's the bear's tracks!"

Jed hurried to him. They stared at the monstrous tracks starkly outlined in caked flour before the gaping doorway.

Mr. Sam crowded between them. "I want to see them bear tracks," he panted.

"Look how big his hind paws are!" Randy said,

holding Mr. Sam back. "They're shaped like a bare-foot man's tracks, a giant man."

"They're grizzly tracks," his father said grimly. He knelt down and spread one big hand over a track. "A good twelve inches long, maybe more. The grizzly that left that track is a monster. And look, the thieving varmint's missing two toes off his left hind paw."

Randy and Mr. Sam squatted down beside their father. "He sure is," Randy muttered.

"Yes, sir, he sure is," Mr. Sam echoed solemnly.

"Reckon lost to a trap?" Randy asked.

"I doubt a trap, not up here in the wilds. More'n likely a fight. One thing for sure, we'll know his track next time we see it."

Molly had come up behind them. "You sure it was a grizzly, Jed?"

"Dead sure. See the way the claws on the front paws reach out a good three inches in front of his toes? Black bears don't leave claw marks like that." He stood up. "Where's Nugget? Where in tarnation did those dogs go?"

"Out the back door," Mr. Sam said placidly. "I reckon they've went after that old grizzly."

Randy jumped to his feet. "Maybe they've picked up his trail."

"Get your gun before you go traipsing after the

dogs," his father said sharply, "and don't get out of earshot."

"Wait, Randy," Mr. Sam bellowed, "wait for me."

"Mr. Sam, you come back here before I tan your britches," Jed hollered.

Randy raced out to his horse and grabbed his rifle out of the boot. He ran around to the back of the cabin. Fifty feet up the slope the dogs were nosing the ground between two big spruce. The boy climbed up to them. They had found the grizzly's tracks in the soft loam. Randy knelt down. Pard crowded against him, whining.

"Tracks too old, boy?" Randy muttered, studying the faint prints of giant paws. He put one arm around the dog.

Pard's tail thumped. He pulled away and moved slowly up the slope, nose rooting the ground, Nugget and Polky snuffling at his heels.

Randy followed the dogs as they worked silently in and around through spruce and pine, climbing higher and higher toward a stand of aspen. A lone pine grew at the edge of the aspen. The dogs snuffled noisily around its trunk. All at once Pard reared up against the tree, nose pointed up. A growl rumbled deep in his chest.

Randy reached the dogs. He stared up at the trunk of the pine. Suddenly he stiffened. Above his head the bark was plastered with dried mud and hair. He backed away from the tree, scanning the ground.

There was the explosive pop of a dead branch behind him. The boy whirled, rifle at shoulder, then went limp. "Pa! You gave me a start. Look, the grizzly's tracks are all around this pine, and see the hair and mud up there on the trunk? It's a rubbing tree. You can see there in the dirt where the grizzly stood up on his hind legs to scratch his back against the trunk."

"With a belly full of vittles from our cabin," Jed said bitterly. "The thieving varmint ought to have been feeling mighty good." His eyes moved slowly up over dried mats of hair and mud. "Look, Randy, way up high there."

Randy stared. High above their heads chunks of bark had been bitten and torn out. The exposed wood was dried and brown. A foot above the wounds, five deeply gouged claw marks stood out dark against the gray trunk.

"He's a monster, that grizzly," Jed muttered.

"Reckon how big, Pa?"

"Seven feet from nose to tail, give six inches."

The boy shivered. "Seven feet," he echoed.

His father turned. "Let's get back. Don't let on to your Ma we found this rubbing tree. No use fretting her. Nugget, you and Pard and Polky come on."

They walked back down to the cabin in silence. Molly sat waiting on the front step. Mr. Sam stood beside her, clutching a rifle as long as he was.

"Well, Jed?" Molly called anxiously.

"Trail was so old it petered out," he said cheerfully.

"Ain't we going to shoot the grizzly?" Mr. Sam demanded.

"We're going to fix up the cabin," Jed said shortly. "Molly, looks like we're going to have to camp out a mite longer."

Mr. Sam propped his rifle against a post and gave his levis a hitch. "You all can sleep out if you want," he growled. "Me, I aim to bed down in the wagon. I don't crave no spooky old grizzly stepping on me, I don't."

His father stood staring at the cabin, rubbing his chin with one thumb. "Randy," he said finally, "you ride back down to the Martins. I saw Henry had a pile of logs and cedar shakes out back of their cabin. Tell him what's happened. He'll loan them to us. You get Hal to help you haul the stuff over in their wagon. Get going."

5 NEIGHBORLY HELP

Toward sunset Randy returned. The Martin clan
came with him. Sarah was on the loaded wagon,
cracking the whip over two black mules. The others
were on horseback. They had brought along food
and bedrolls. While the men and boys unloaded the
lumber, the women set up camp under the spruce.

They were at work before sunup next morning.

All that day they labored. By noon of the second day they were finished. Jed stood in the middle of the floor and surveyed the cabin with satisfaction. The staples hauled up from Texas were laid out on new shelves beside the cooking hearth. Molly's rocking chair was drawn up before the fireplace. Randy and Hal had fashioned a table of boards laid over saw-horses and had nailed together a long bench for each side. Feather beds were fluffed in the two double wall bunks. Clothes hung neatly from wall pegs.

"We never could have done it without you folks," Jed told Henry gratefully.

"Would just have taken longer," Henry replied. "Well, Jed, what do we do next?"

"Do next?" Jed asked in surprise. "Raise cows. What else?"

Sarah Martin stalked over to them, arms akimbo. "But what about the grizzly that tore this cabin up?" she demanded. "Ain't you going to try to get him before he does more devilment?"

"Sarah, that grizzly's tracks are a couple weeks old, at least," Jed told her. "The dogs couldn't trail him, even if I wanted so."

"You do aim to use your dogs on bear, don't you?" Henry asked. "I know you said they're ketch dogs, but after all—"

"Henry," Jed said deliberately, "I aim to use the dogs for ketch dogs, nothing else."

"But Jed, there ain't any wild cows for them to catch."

Jed walked over and sat down on the bench by the table. "The only reason I'm telling you this, Henry, is we're close neighbors, and out here in the wilds, close neighbors have got to stick together, right?"

"Right," Henry nodded.

"Well, then, you ever hear about a vanished long-horn herd up here in the Big Horns?"

"You mean that Texas herd Indians stampeded a few years back? Everybody knows about them. Nobody's ever laid eyes on a one of them cows since."

"I have. Part of that herd ranges in the timber around here, Henry. I ran onto a bunch last year when I was hunting in this very canyon."

Henry's eyebrows shot up. "So that's how come you moved up here with just fifty head of longhorns. And why you brought along ketch dogs. You aim to build you up a herd catching wild cows."

"Exactly, Henry. We've settled in grizzly country, but I sure didn't come out here to start no war with them. I aim to live peaceable with them, much as I can. I sure don't aim to risk getting my dogs killed by no bear. Our whole future depends on those dogs. If we lost them, we'd be licked before we got good started."

He turned to Sarah Martin. "You don't have to be afraid, Sarah," he said earnestly. "Grizzlies for the most part are wary critters. They'll do more'n their share to keep out of sight of humans. But you and Henry—and all of us—we've got to keep in mind there's danger everywhere out here in the wilds. We're going to be living with danger at our doorsteps, and we've got to be on guard every minute."

"Did you ever hunt a grizzly, Mr. Reynolds?" Hal Martin asked eagerly.

"Once, Hal. It was when I was out here last year after buffalo. I went out on a grizzly trail with an old bear hunter, fellow by the name of Ben Waters. Ben, he'd hunted grizzlies nigh onto thirty years. Wasn't a trick he didn't know. Had a pack of grizzly dogs, five of them. Hounds. Blue Ticks and Red Bones, mostly."

"Tell them what happened, Pa," Randy urged.

"Me and Ben trailed a grizzly four days over the roughest canyons in the Big Horns," Jed told them. "Lost the dogs the third day. Couldn't keep up with them."

"Did you ever find them?" Hal asked.

"We found them, all right. Under a cliff, dead. They'd bayed the grizzly, and he'd killed every last dog. I felt sorry as the dickens for old Ben. He'd trained those dogs from pups. I helped him bury them under the cliff. Then we walked a day and a night back to camp, Ben not saying a word."

Henry shook his head, lips tight. "Much as I craved Wyoming grass, I doubt I'd ever have homesteaded here if I'd realized how thick the grizzlies are," he said somberly. "I've heard bad talk about grizzlies killing cows."

"I've heard tall tales, too, Henry, but it just don't stand to reason a grizzly'd bother much with cows out here, not with the Big Horns full of easy game."

"Of course, I've got bear traps," Henry said reflectively. "Reckon I could set them out around our place."

"I wouldn't bother, Henry, not unless the bears give you real trouble. Old Ben, he didn't set too much store by traps. Claimed grizzlies were too smart to get caught."

"But what's a fellow to do?"

Jed got up. "Just like I said a while ago. Be careful. When you're in timber, take care you don't ride on to a grizzly and spook him. That's the only time you're likely to get in trouble. Me and Randy, now, we've got more chance for trouble than you all, seeing we'll be after wild cows in timber most of the time, and in strange country, too. I figure we'll be running across bear trails. I aim to learn where the grizzlies range and where they den up. For the rest, I aim to give them a wide berth."

"How do you figure on setting about tracking down the wild cows, Jed?"

"Well, Henry, to catch wild cows a brush popper needs three things: a good horse and ketch dogs and neck oxen."

"Neck oxen?"

"Like our Pancho and Pablo. Don't you be fooled, Henry, just because you saw them pull our wagon up here. Pancho and Pablo are trained to bring in wild cows we rope to them neck and neck."

"I don't follow you, Jed."

"Well, it's this way. The dogs track down a wild cow and flush it out of timber. When they get it in an open spot, we rope it. Then we tie the cow to a good-sized sapling with a tie rope."

Jed stepped over to a wall peg and took down a stout seven-foot rope. "This here is a tie rope. Once that cow is tied, all it can do is go round and round the tree till it's plumb worn out."

"Takes a couple of days," Randy added. "When the cow doesn't have much fight left, we take up a neck ox and rope the cow to the ox and turn them loose. The ox will drag that cow home to the corral straight as the crow flies every single time."

"The ox knows he'll get a bait of oats once he's fetched the wild critter safe home," Jed added dryly.

"Danged if it don't sound like a smart trick," Henry told him. "What you aiming to use for your corral, Jed?"

"Going to fence off the mouth of a side canyon about a hundred yards down east of the cabin here. It's got walls straight up and down and a little creek. It'll make a prime trap pasture for holding the wild critters till they gentle down enough to turn out with the herd."

Henry stretched tiredly. "You're welcome to the wild cow business, Jed. Plain, ordinary, range-broke stock is good enough for me. Well, Mama, we best light out for home, now things are tidied up here."

"Not without you eat dinner," Molly protested.

"We best get started," he refused. "We've been away two days. With all this grizzly talk, I feel my mind'll rest easier if me and Hal ride over our range and check our cows."

Early in the afternoon thunderheads gathered around Mt. Baldy. The sky darkened. Thunder rumbled. Lightning forked through the sky. The rain came suddenly, a cold, hard, driving rain from out of the west that sent Randy scurrying out to the porch for an armload of firewood he and Hal had cut and stacked that morning.

Jed built up the fire and they gathered around it, Molly in her rocking chair, Jed and the boys on the floor.

"Lordy, but it's good to have a stout roof over our heads and a fire crackling in the fireplace," Jed sighed.

They rested, contented, while the rain drummed on the roof. The rain slacked off in half an hour. Jed stirred, stretched lazily.

"How'd you all like to walk down and have a look at that side canyon I'm aiming to make into a trap pasture?"

Mr. Sam scrambled up and ran to the window. "The rain's done let up," he shouted. "The sky's getting blue. Let's go." He started for the door.

"Hold on there, Mr. Sam," his mother told him. "You just hold your horses. We'll go together."

The dogs came out from under the porch as they stepped out of the cabin. The sun was out. Whisky-jacks whistled raucously from dripping spruce boughs. Down in Bear Claw Canyon, steam swirls rose from wet grass. Along the stream the longhorns grazed contentedly.

They set out down canyon, the boys leading the way. Molly slipped her arm through Jed's. She drew a deep breath. "The air's so clean," she told him. "That spicy smell from the spruce and pine makes me feel good clear down to my toes."

"You do like our canyon, don't you, girl?"

"I love it," she said simply. "Once I get the cabin to rights and get the wash done, I aim to saddle Mesquite and ride all over it. Look, Jed, see that clump of cottonwoods there down by the stream? They were the first thing caught my eye when you brought us into the canyon."

"You sure had me worried that day," he confessed. "I couldn't rightly tell what you were thinking."

"Silly." She gave his arm a squeeze. "Oh, look at the sun sparkling the snow on Baldy and on that peak beyond, the one there to the east."

"Henry was saying yesterday that Indians call that one Lobo Peak, though he claims there ain't no wolf packs hereabouts any more."

"Did he tell you the names of the other mountains?" Randy broke in.

His father nodded. "That big one straight down east at the end of our canyon is Eagle Mountain, and the one back up this way on the north side is Bear Tooth, on account of it's shaped like a tooth out of a bear's bottom jaw. Our cabin's on the slope of Moccasin, but don't ask me why it's named that, because Henry didn't know."

"What about the peak back up west, the one that flanks the Martin ranch?" Randy asked.

"That's Elk Mountain," Jed replied.

"I hope it lives up to its name," Molly told him. "That haunch of venison Sarah gave us won't last us long."

They had reached the mouth of the side canyon. Jed led the way inside. They walked up along the bank of the mountain brook that gurgled down over smooth white pebbles on its way to join the stream in the main canyon. The box canyon was not more than a hundred feet wide and five hundred deep. Perpendicular rock cliffs towered a hundred feet high on three sides.

"Fence across the mouth, and we'll have us a trap pasture that'll hold any wild longhorns we bring in," Jed said with satisfaction. "I never saw a better place to gentle wild cows."

"I know there's plenty of water," Randy said worriedly, "but reckon there's grass enough?"

"Don't want too much. When we get a bunch gentled, we'll turn them out to graze with our herd. If they're gaunted down, they won't hightail it back to the mountains. I figure that way, we'll be able to hold them."

6 THE WILD COW

Jed and Randy started work on the canyon corral at sunup next day. All that day they labored at digging a trench three feet deep across the mouth of the side canyon. The next day they took axes and saw and climbed the slope above the cabin to a stand of young pines. For two days they felled trees, trimming off branches, sawing trunks into ten-foot lengths. Molly and Mr. Sam rode up on Mesquite and Poca and snaked the logs down to the corral at the ends of lariats tied to their saddle horns.

On the fourth day, the fence was finished. Seven feet tall, the logs were set vertically in the trench, hammered close together, the earth tamped hard and firm around their base. As an added safeguard Jed soaked a cowhide he had brought up from Texas and when it was soft, sliced it into stout strips with his bowie knife, then lashed the logs together five feet above ground.

"Soon as that cowhide dries out, it'll hold like iron," he told Randy with satisfaction. "We've done a good job. You know, I've got it in my mind to call this corral the Little Brasada. Makes me think of Texas, somehow."

"That's a good name, Pa. You aiming for us to start looking for the vanished longhorns, now we're done here?"

His father nodded. "We'll take the dogs out in the morning and scout around for tracks. Reckon we'll take Mr. Sam along. He's been cooped up too much."

They were in the saddle by sunup next morning. Jed looked disapprovingly at Mr. Sam. The youngster's chubby legs were too short for the stirrups. They stuck straight out from Poca's sides.

"Get your feet in those stirrup loops," Jed ordered. "We don't want you taking a tumble, young man."

"Pooh, I won't fall off," Mr. Sam scoffed, but he wedged his boots into the loops obediently.

"Look for us when you see us coming," Jed called to Molly, who stood watching from the cabin door.

"I'll have a johnnycake ready for supper," she promised, waving good-by.

Jed whistled to the dogs and they set out. Down in the canyon the dark shapes of cattle were shrouded in layers of mist. As they rode by a spruce, a bird twittered sleepily.

They passed the Little Brasada and headed east. Timbered slopes gave way to upjutting cliffs indented by box canyons.

"When I was up here last summer, I never rightly took time to ride the whole valley," Jed told the boys. "We want to find which of the side canyons have got water. That's where we'll find game trails. And where there's game trails, chances are we'll find our wild cow tracks."

Patiently they rode the canyon wall in and out of side canyons. They were more than two hours reaching the steep slope of Eagle Mountain at the east end of Bear Claw Canyon. When they reached the stream, they rode out into the water and reined up to let horses and dogs drink.

"What do you aim to name our creek, Pa?" Randy asked over the rush and roar of water.

"Got any good ideas?"

Randy hesitated. "What about Grizzly Creek?"

"Grizzly Creek," Jed repeated slowly. "Sounds good."

"Grizzly Creek," Mr. Sam echoed with thoughtful scowl. "Well now, I reckon Grizzly Creek suits me."

His father and brother exchanged glances. "If it's all right by Mr. Sam, then Grizzly Creek it is," Jed said solemnly, and so it was settled.

They rode up out of the stream and headed for the south wall of the canyon, riding slowly, scanning the cliffs.

"We've been in a dozen side canyons," Randy told his father. "Looks like there just ain't any game trails."

"We've still got half our canyon to ride," Jed said shortly. "We'll find them."

It took them the better part of an hour to reach Lobo Peak. They were riding along under its jutting precipices when Mr. Sam spoke up. "I'm hungry," he said flatly.

His father glared at him. "And you whine because

we don't bring you along more. You'll eat when we get home."

Mr. Sam gave him a lopsided grin. "You and Randy be good boys," he chuckled, "and I'll give you some of my grub." He reached into his saddlebag and hauled out a package wrapped in white cloth. "Ma, she figured I'd get hungry."

"Well, I'll be—" his father broke off. "Say, that meat and bread looks pretty good. Don't mind if I do have a bite. Randy?"

They rode along munching the meat and bread. Lobo Peak dropped behind them. They were following a cliff at the base of a saddle ridge which stretched all the way west to Mt. Baldy. As they rounded a jutting promontory, they rode onto the wide mouth of a timbered canyon which tunneled back into the ridge between steeply sloping sides.

Jed reined up. "This looks likely," he said, excitement edging his voice. "We ought to find a game trail coming down in there." He whistled up the dogs. "Randy, you follow me and the dogs. Mr. Sam, keep back of your brother. No talking, now."

Horses and dogs threaded in and out through crowded pines which blanketed the floor of the canyon. Under the trees light filtered down palely. The only sound was the muffled thud of hoofs on the thick carpet of pine needles. Then Randy caught the muted gurgle of water. He cocked his ear, straining to locate the sound.

Suddenly there came a loud grating noise from the timber ahead. They reined up. The dogs froze, noses high.

Randy held his breath. The grating, gnawing sound was like nothing he had ever heard. He looked at his father. Jed sat listening, brow knitted. Randy glanced back at Mr. Sam. The little fellow sat his horse openmouthed.

Then all at once the harsh grating ceased. There was a moment's silence, then an explosive crack, a resounding splash, and all was quiet again.

"What was it?" Mr. Sam bleated.

"Shh!" his father whispered. For a moment longer he listened, then turned and looked at Randy. "It was a tree falling," he said in a low voice. "and into water. Funny thing, though, there's no wind to blow a tree down." He slid his rifle out of the saddle boot. "Mr. Sam, mind you stay back of your brother. Nugget, go get 'em!"

The dogs tore out through the timber, not tonguing. Jed spurred Corker after them, Pepper and Poca close on his heels. Randy slid his rifle out of its boot as he rode. The boy chewed at his lip. He was sweating.

All at once he saw his father rein up. Randy rode

up alongside him, sat staring. They were at the edge of a large park. In the center lay a wide green pool, dammed up by a curving line of mud-plastered sticks and branches and logs. Water trickled through the dam, forming into a narrow runoff flowing down toward the mouth of the canyon. The banks of the pool were dotted with pointed white aspen stumps.

Randy's eyes riveted on the big aspen that had just toppled half into the pool. Its fragile leaves still trembled. All at once there was a flurry of movement among the leaves, a loud gnawing sound.

Mr. Sam crowded Poca up alongside Pepper. "What is it?" the little fellow squealed. "What's that noise?"

At the sound of his voice there came a sudden streak of brown from out of the aspen boughs, a splash, then a loud slapping whack against water. The still surface of the pool broke into ripples.

The dogs raced toward the fallen tree, barking excitedly. "Beaver!" Jed exclaimed. "Doggone it, Mr. Sam, if you hadn't sounded off, we might could have seen him."

Mr. Sam hung his head, bottom lip quivering. "Reckon I got a mite spooked," he said in a small voice.

"Big boys don't spook so easy," his father said scathingly. "Look at those fool dogs smelling over those stumps, Randy. That beaver smell's got them plumb puzzled."

Randy touched Pepper forward along the east bank of the pool. When he reached the dogs he reined up and leaned down from the saddle. Suddenly he let out a whoop. "Pa, bear tracks! A black bear's been messing around the pond."

Jed rode toward the pool. Mr. Sam did not budge.

"By heck, you're right," Jed told Randy. "Cooking grease! Look at the dogs. Those bear tracks are hot."

"We going to trail him?" Randy asked eagerly.

His father shook his head. "Reckon not," he said regretfully. "Be too risky, with Mr. Sam along. He'd spook us for sure."

From where he sat Poca, the little fellow heard. His chin trembled. Blindly he swung the paint mare around and rode slowly through the shallow runoff below the pool and up the west bank. All at once he reined up and leaned down along Poca's neck. "Pa!" he bellowed, "Pa! Cow tracks!"

Jed and Randy came at a gallop. They splashed through the runoff and reined up beside the paint mare. "Mr. Sam's right!" Jed exclaimed. "Our first wild cow tracks!"

The dogs came racing at his whistle. They snuffled noisily along the deep cleft prints, tails twitching.

Jed nudged Corker after them until the cow tracks vanished at a seepage water at the edge of the timber. Calling the dogs, he turned back.

"Tracks are too old," he announced, "but there's bound to be a trail coming down somewhere in the canyon." He looked longingly toward the big pines beyond the pond. "We daren't go into timber looking for it, not with Mr. Sam along. We'll have to take him back to the cabin. That'll still leave us daylight enough to find the trail."

"I don't want to go back," Mr. Sam wailed. "They're my cow tracks, ain't they? I found them, didn't I? I don't want to go back, Pa, honest."

Jed rubbed his chin with his thumb. "It oughtn't to take us more'n two shakes to find the trail," he said slowly. "You reckon you can sit your horse here at the dam and keep out of trouble that long?"

"Sure I can. I'll watch for the beaver. I won't budge out of the clearing, cross my heart."

"You do, and I'll tan your britches good. Polky, stay with Mr. Sam. Ready, Randy? Pard, Nugget, come on."

They rode up past the beaver pond, then swung off to the right into timber. No tracks showed on the thick carpet of pine needles. The dogs fanned out ahead, snuffling over the ground. Then Pard let out a sharp yelp as he came upon a mound of cow dung under a tree. The dogs were off.

Jed and Randy sent their horses at a run after them, dodging from side to side to miss the slap of pine boughs. For a hundred yards they followed hard on the dogs. Then a dense thicket of pine saplings loomed up ahead. The dogs dropped to their bellies, worming their way into the brush. The horses crashed breast on into the heavy growth.

Randy dropped down along Pepper's neck, pressing his face against the rough mane. For a few yards he took a beating. Then abruptly the slash of branches ceased. Under him Pepper slowed, stopped. Randy pushed erect. They had ridden out onto an old game trail. The dogs were away up the trail, their excited voices rolling back.

"Old elk trail," Jed said happily. "See the cow tracks there? Wild cows are using the trail, all right. I bet the critters follow it clean back down to the beaver pond."

"Listen to the dogs, Pa. They're on a hot trail."

"And we can't follow it, not and leave Mr. Sam back there." He stuck two fingers to his mouth and let out a piercing whistle. In a moment the dogs came streaking back down the trail. They slid to a stop and gazed up at Jed and Randy with uneasy whines.

"They think I've gone plumb crazy, calling them

back," Jed said. "Let's get Mr. Sam home and come back up here."

As they swung their horses back down the trail, they heard the faint barking of a dog. They reined up.

"That's Polky," Jed said uneasily.

Beside him Pard growled deep in his chest, hackles bristling. Nugget whined. The distant barking broke off. For a moment the timber was still. Then there came the terrified scream of a child, thin and shrill.

"Mr. Sam!" Jed shouted, hitting Corker with the spurs. The sorrel leaped forward into a run.

Randy sent Pepper after him. The dogs were out ahead, bellies low to the ground as they sped down the trail. The timber faded past in a gray blur. All at once, above the pound of hoofs, Jed and Randy heard the bellow of a cow. The next moment the horses skidded around a sharp curve and out into the clearing beside the dam.

They reined to a sliding stop. The clearing looked empty.

"Mr. Sam!" Jed shouted. "Mr. Sam!"

His shout was echoed by the angry bellow of a cow, the shrill barking of a dog. Jed and Randy sent the horses splashing through the runoff. Pard and Nugget were already across and up beyond the dam. All at once Randy gave a shout. There was Poca, rearing and plunging at the end of the lariat which tethered her fast to an aspen. Between the terrified mare and the pond Mr. Sam scrouged against an aspen stump, a tiny bawling white calf half lifted in his arms. Ten feet away a snorting, bellowing long-horn cow pawed the ground, shaking wicked horns at the darting blur of dog harassing her with shrill barks.

Suddenly the cow lowered her head and charged. Cruel twisted horns came around in a vicious swipe at Polky, missed. The maddened cow backed up, bellowing deafeningly. Polky dodged in under her horns.

Jed and Randy had lariats shaken out as they thundered up. They swung out wide around the cow and dog, ropes ready. They got no chance to throw. Pard and Nugget hit the cow from behind, barking wildly, teeth snapping at her heels.

The cow whirled to meet the new enemy. Pard was inside her horns. With a leap he sank his teeth in her nose, then squatted, muscles bulging in massive shoulders. His big head snapped around in a sharp twist, his body swinging. The cow fell to the ground, feet flailing.

Before she was down, Jed and Randy were on the ground. "Around her horns!" Jed hollered. He jerked a short rope from his belt. "I'll hog-tie."

In the moment the cow lay stunned, Randy had his rope around the outspread horns. He jerked it tight. Out of the corner of his eye he saw his father sitting on the cow's rump, giving the last pull to a three-leg cross tie. Then Jed got up, breathing heavily.

"Leave go, Pard," he panted.

Randy jumped back as Pard let go of the cow's nose and rolled clear. The cow came alive, bellowing, rolling from side to side.

"Get on Pepper," Jed ordered. "Haul her over to that aspen there."

Randy swung into the saddle. He checked the knotted rope on the saddle horn, then touched Pepper forward. Under his knees he felt the stallion's muscles ripple as the roan strained against the cow's weight. Then Pepper had her moving, was dragging her over the ground.

Jed followed, a tie rope in his hands. "Whoa," he hollered. "That's good. Hold her right there."

Quickly he threw the rope around the cow's horns and tied a double cross knot in front. Then he brought the loose ends around the tree, sliding the double round knot on one end through the slipknot on the other and pulling it tight. With one deft move he loosed Randy's rope and jerked it free.

"Take the horses back out of the way," he ordered.

When they were clear he stooped and untied the rope holding the cow's feet. She lunged to her feet. With earsplitting bellows she went around and around the tree, backing, pulling, butting. The tie rope held firm.

"Good job," Jed panted, wiping his sweaty face with his sleeve. He looked around. "Where's the young hellion that started this?"

Mr. Sam stepped out from the shelter of the stump, dragging the bawling calf. He looked up at his father with frightened eyes.

Seeing her calf, the wild cow redoubled her bellows. Jed snatched the calf from Mr. Sam and pushed it within reach of its mother. For a moment the cow left off bellowing, nosing the calf frantically, licking it roughly.

"I ought to tan your hide!" Jed snapped at Mr. Sam.

Mr. Sam stuck out his chin. "I didn't set foot out of the clearing, just like you said," he protested. "I figured you'd be proud, me hearing the calf bawling and finding it all by myself. Course, Polky helped some," he added honestly.

His father raised his hands, dropped them helplessly.

"Why'd you go and give my calf back to its

mammy?" Mr. Sam said aggrievedly. "I aimed to tote that calf home."

"You know better than monkey around with wild longhorns," Jed said in a strangled voice. "You came in an inch of getting yourself killed."

"I want my calf back," Mr. Sam said stubbornly. "I aim—"

"Hush your mouth and get on your horse," Jed shouted. "That calf stays with its mammy till we bring out a neck ox and take them both in."

7 VANISHED LONGHORNS

Next morning Jed and Randy were in the saddle by dawn. They rode out across the still canyon leading Pancho, the neck ox, the three dogs trotting silently in their wake. Fleecy clouds drifted down the gray of the sky. As they neared the beaver canyon, the craggy peak of Eagle Mountain stood out starkly against the crimson of the rising sun.

74

Light filtered down thinly through the trees at the edge of the clearing around the beaver pond. The wild cow stood spraddle-legged, head down, calf nuzzling her flank. The cow glared balefully, but put up no fight when Jed and Randy tied her neck and neck to Pancho. When Jed lifted her bawling calf and slung it across in front of his saddle, however, the cow set up a loud bellowing. They started for home, Pancho dragging the bellowing cow close behind the horses.

An hour later, Jed and Randy turned cow and calf loose in the new canyon corral. They turned Pancho out and rode back across the canyon and up to the beaver pond, then swung onto the old game trail where they had found cow tracks the day before. The dogs trotted out in front of the horses, heads high.

They climbed steadily, winding in and around through thick stands of pine. High above the pond the timber began to thin. They rode out at last into an open park ringed with tall pines, their trunks rising like straight columns. Grass grew high in the clearing.

Jed and Randy reined up. On the far side of the park stretched a curving wall of perpendicular cliffs. As Randy scanned the scattering of pines at the base, he felt Pepper's muscles ripple under his legs. He glanced down, saw the stallion's ears prick forward. The boy looked at the dogs. They were standing tense, hackles rising.

"Over there," his father hissed. "To your right."

Randy turned. A hundred feet to the west, twenty or thirty wild longhorns stood belly-deep in grass, tails in air, heads high toward the riders. Sunlight glinted off outspreading horns.

"They've spotted us," Jed muttered. "Look sharp."

Suddenly the longhorns wheeled with one motion and bolted west toward timber.

"Get 'em!" Jed hollered, and the dogs flashed across the park, lunging through long grass, vanishing into the timber on the heels of the longhorns.

"Shake the kinks out of your rope, Son," Jed said quietly. "The dogs'll have them back."

Randy obeyed, hands shaking as the dogs tongued. He could feel the thump of Pepper's heart under his legs. The boy licked dry lips.

Suddenly a surging line of bellowing cows came plunging back out into the clearing, the barking, nipping dogs at their heels. Then Pard came streaking up along the flank, barking, jumping, butting, forcing the line into a wide swing toward Jed and Randy.

With wild yippees, they spurred to meet the cows.

The longhorns braked, wheeled, raced south toward timber at the base of the cliff. Ropes snaked out. Loops settled over the horns of two heifers. Corker and Pepper squatted against the jerk. The heifers hit the ends of the ropes. Hoofs flew up. The heifers crashed to the ground with frantic bawls. Dogs and cows swept past and vanished into the timber beyond.

Jed and Randy raced against time. They hog-tied the heifers and dragged them over to pines, tying them fast. From the timber came the bawling of cattle, the barking of dogs.

"Hit the saddle," Jed hollered. "The dogs are swinging them back."

The next moment the dogs hazed the bellowing longhorns back out into the park. The horses lunged forward, pounding up along the flank of the tight bunch. Jed threw, then Randy. Two cows crashed to the ground. The dogs raced away west into the trees on the heels of the panicked cattle.

Jed and Randy had the stunned cows hog-tied. "Any brand on yours?" Jed panted.

Randy shook his head.

"Then they were calved after the herd got spooked by Indians," Jed said with satisfaction. He took off his Stetson and wiped his sweaty brow. "Whew! We were lucky. Chances are, we'll never get four in one day again. Say, can you hear the dogs, Randy?"

"Sure can't, Pa."

When they had tied the bawling cows to pines, they climbed back into the saddle. "Those fool dogs have gone plumb crazy," Jed growled. "Been away from cow catching too long. Likely chase those spooked longhorns all over creation. Come on, there's bound to be a cow trail leading out somewhere."

Where the wild longhorns had stampeded west into timber the grass was trampled, the turf cut by hoofs. Jed and Randy followed the tracks through the ring of pines. In the timber the cows had swung sharp to the left. Jed and Randy rode onto a cow trail some ten feet short of the cliff, a narrow, hard-packed trail which wound away between the timber and the curving wall of rock.

They swung west onto the trail, Jed in the lead. Randy gazed about curiously. On their left, sprawling talus slides sloped down from the cliff. In the timber on their right, thick aspen clumps thrust slender white trunks up between arching pine boughs.

For over a mile they followed the cow trail along the base of the cliff. The sun beat down hot. Randy gave a sigh of relief when the cliff ended abruptly in a tumbled mass of big boulders. The trail made a sharp turn south around the stacked-up rocks. For a moment Randy lost sight of his father. Then, as Pepper rounded the point, Randy saw him.

Jed had reined up. Silently he motioned Randy to a halt. While their horses shifted nervously, saddles creaking, they gazed in astonishment out across a little glade to where a dozen or more big longhorns had broken off grazing to stare.

Jed and Randy watched, scarcely breathing. Except for a slow bunching, the longhorns made no move. They stood belly-deep in high grass, heads and tails in air, long curved horns bobbing and jerking.

"Bulls!" Jed whispered. "Not a cow in the bunch!"

For long, breathless moments bulls and men faced each other. Then from the center of the bunch a bull stepped forward, big black head high, dewlap swaying, white rump spots glistening against glossy black hide. The big head wobbled under the weight of massive, outswept horns.

Jed drew a deep breath. "What a bull," he whispered. "What a bull. And us without a dog."

"Look at that right horn," Randy murmured. "See how straight up it hooks? He'd be a mean one, that bull."

"He makes old Stomper look runty," Jed muttered. "I'm going to have that black devil. I know it'd be crazy to tackle him without the dogs—" he broke off and sat chewing at his lip, watching the bull.

Fifty feet from the horses the bull halted. Fascinated, Randy gazed at the flare of black nostrils, the wild stare of baleful eyes. "You want we should try, Pa?" he whispered. "If you'll head, I'll heel. We can bust him flat."

His father eased his rope free, testing the tie on the saddle horn. "If we don't try now, might be we'd never get another chance," he muttered. "Get set."

At that moment the black bull snorted, wheeled, and broke into a run back into the bunch. That spooked the lot. They scattered, stampeded west for timber, tails high.

"Let's go!" Jed hollered, jabbing Corker with his spurs.

They galloped across the glade. At the edge they reined up. The bulls had vanished into timber. They could hear the crash of brush in the distance. Dust hung thick under the trees.

"There's bound to be a trail somewhere," Jed muttered. "Come on."

Within a hundred feet they rode upon four diverging cow trails. Jed reined up, shoving his Stetson to the back of his head.

"Which one?" Randy asked.

"Likely they all head for the same pasture. We'll take the wide one there."

The trail climbed steeply, winding around and up through thick stands of lodgepole pine. Bushy-tailed squirrels streaked up and down tree trunks. From the treetops whisky-jacks scolded noisily. Corker and Pepper stepped cautiously over low windfalls which blocked the steep trail. By the time they had climbed five hundred yards, both horses were blowing.

Jed twisted around in the saddle. "Pull up for a minute," he called.

High overhead the pine tops moaned and sighed in the wind. Suddenly over the sound, over the raspy wheezes of the horses, came a hoarse, croaking chorus which swelled louder and louder. Jed and Randy peered up through the pine boughs. A dark shadow moved between them and the sky. A huge flock of black birds flashed overhead. The air was loud with coarse caws, grunts, screams. The horses whinnied with fright, rearing, straining at the bit.

"Easy, Pepper," Randy cried. "Pa, what are they?"

"Ravens," Jed shouted, fighting Corker down. He gave the horse his head. The big sorrel lunged up the trail, hoofs scattering rocks. Randy sent Pepper after him. With a loud beating of wings the ravens sailed along overhead, croaking dismally.

The trail bent sharply to the right. The horses labored up and around. Sunlight opened up on a park fifty feet ahead. At the edge of the clearing a big blowdown blocked the trail. The horses were almost upon it when all at once there came a puff of wind from out of the west. The stinking smell of carrion hit Jed's and Randy's noses. At the same moment a dozen ravens rose from beyond the blowdown, beating the air with heavy wings, croaking, cawing.

Jed and Randy reined up. "There's some kind of carcass on the far side of that blowdown," Jed told the boy, wrinkling his nose. "Let's have a look."

They dismounted and led the horses around the tangle of dead branches. Overhead the ravens circled screaming. Suddenly Corker and Pepper snorted and jerked back against the reins. On the trampled ground beside the blowdown was the bloody, half-eaten carcass of a mule deer buck. Most of the belly had been devoured. One haunch was gone. Huge chunks of flesh had been ripped from the chest.

Keeping tight hold of Pepper's reins, Randy squatted down beside the stinking carcass. "Something broke the buck's back," he said excitedly. "Look how his backbone's poking out through the flesh." He got up and stepped around the carcass.

Suddenly he stopped. "Pa," he cried, "come here quick! A grizzly killed the buck! Here's his tracks!"

Jed dropped Corker's reins and ran to Randy's side. He stared down at plate-sized tracks pressed deep in black loam. In front of the toe marks were the curved marks of long claws.

"They're the same shape as the grizzly tracks in our cabin," Randy cried, "only not near so big."

Jed nodded. "This was a sow grizzly, that's why. See those small tracks there amongst the big ones? The sow had a cub with her."

Stooping, he walked slowly along the back tracks of the grizzly and her cub. Fifteen feet beyond the carcass he stopped and straightened up. "These are fresh tracks. Not a speck of dust in them. It's God's mercy we didn't ride onto that grizzly while she was feeding. If you happen on a grizzly in timber, chances are the bear will turn tail and run. But if you spook a grizzly while it's feeding—especially a sow with cubs—" he broke off, shaking his head.

Randy shivered. He glanced nervously about the clearing.

"We've got to keep our eyes peeled," his father went on. "We're in grizzly territory. For every sow grizzly with a cub, there's a male grizzly somewhere about. Watch sharp, Randy. There's no telling when we might ride on one without warning."

He started toward his horse. "Come on, we've lost too much time already from catching up with that black bull."

As they rode away up the trail the ravens still circled in the air, croaking, screaming. Slowly their din faded.

The trail steepened. Timber thinned. The ground was crusted with shelving rock that rang under the horses' hoofs. With a final spurt, Corker and Pepper topped out onto a flat divide. Jed and Randy reined up. They were on a tabletop covered with grass and scattered clumps of scrubby cedar.

Randy gazed out across the flat. On the far side he could see the tops of big spruce thrusting up from below the tabletop. In the distance beyond the treetops a craggy mountain towered, its steep side checkered by open meadows and heavy stands of timber.

The boy's gaze wandered over the high meadows. Suddenly he gave a low cry. "Pa! Up there on the mountain! Cows!"

Jed half rose in his stirrups. "The vanished longhorns!" he shouted. "Randy, the vanished longhorns! Come on! We've got to find a way up to them!"

They spurred their horses out through high grass. Suddenly Randy gave a warning shout and reined Pepper back on his haunches.

"What's the matter with you?" Jed hollered, jerking Corker to a sliding stop.

"Rocks in the grass ahead. Big ones."

"Circle around. Keep going!"

Randy sent Pepper around the jagged outcroppings. Fifty yards beyond, the tabletop fell away in a steep slope thickly timbered with spruce. They reined up.

Jed scanned the timbered drop-off. "There, to the west, Randy. A cow trail leading down."

"There's two trails down there to the east," Randy pointed, "and—" the boy broke off, lifting up in his stirrups. "Pa! Through that gap! Look!"

Through a gap in the spruce they stared straight down into a wide oval valley, carpeted with lush grass streaked with bright sweeps of wildflowers. Longhorns were everywhere. They grazed belly-deep in the grass, their sharp, high backs dun and black and white and red. They stood knee-deep out in a narrow stream, long tails switching idly. They bunched in the shade of tall spruce along the edge of the meadow.

Jed made a sound deep in his throat. "The valley of the vanished longhorns," he whispered. "Kind Father in Heaven, we've found them."

Randy looked at his father's rapt face. He licked

his lips nervously. "There's a thousand of them, Pa!"

Jed shook his head, not looking at the boy. "Not near that many," he said slowly, "but they're ours, ours for the taking. Randy, you and I'll build up a herd like nothing in this whole territory. Jed Reynolds and Sons, that's what we'll call our outfit. Jed Reynolds and Sons. Not brush poppers, Randy. Cattlemen! Cattlemen of Wyoming!"

8 THE BLOOD CALL

They sat watching the longhorns until the sky in the west was tinged with red. A cold wind had sprung up out of the north. In the meadow, bunches of wild longhorns started walking toward the pines below the ridge where Jed and Randy sat their horses.

Jed stirred, glanced over his shoulder. "Sun's

already back of Baldy. I hate to leave those longhorns out of my sight, but we best hit the trail for home."

They swung their horses around and headed back across the tabletop. At the edge Randy held Pepper back, giving Corker room. Then they were down onto the cow trail, the horses leaning back on their haunches against the steep grade.

They came down onto a little flat and reined up.

"Have you figured out how we're going to tackle that herd?" Randy asked his father.

"I've been turning it over in my mind," Jed said slowly. "It'll take—" Jed never finished the sentence. His words were drowned out by a blood-curdling bellow trumpeting higher and higher into a drawn-out bawling scream.

"Pa! What was it?" Randy cried; then, "Pepper! Easy, easy, there, boy!"

The roan stallion had reared, whinnying, fore-hoofs pawing the air. Randy fought him down. His father was having his own troubles. Corker's head was down between front legs. Hind legs lashed out.

Jed sawed at the reins, forcing the sorrel's head up. "Whoa, boy, whoa," he panted. "It was a bull, Randy, a bull in trouble."

At that moment a deep-throated roar ripped down from the high ridge they had just quit. Jed's head jerked up. "Bear!" he shouted, yanking Corker around, raking him with the spurs. "A bear's after that bull!"

Corker lunged back up the trail, crowding Pepper off into brush. The roan's ears flattened. His back humped. "Pepper!" Randy shouted. "Easy, boy, easy down!"

He got the roan turned, then let him go. Pepper stretched out low, lunging up the steep grade and out onto the tabletop. In half a dozen strides he pulled up alongside Corker.

Jed had swung left, was spurring the sorrel straight west toward a stand of tall pines. "Where those ravens are circling!" he shouted, wind whipping his words away.

They spurred at a dead run down through the brush. Over the pound of hoofs Randy could hear furious bellows, savage roars. Wind stung the boy's eyes. He swiped at them with his sleeve, glancing across at his father. Jed was riding low on Corker's neck, his face grim.

The horses crashed headlong into a dense growth of scrubby cedar. They were close on the pines now. Randy could see the ravens, see them swoop low over the trees, glossy black wings almost fanning the treetops.

The boy squinted against the wind. Suddenly there was a wild bellow so close that Pepper almost jumped out from under him. Randy grabbed for the saddle horn, flinching as a hoarse roar drowned out the bellow. At that moment Pepper whistled in terror and hunkered back on his haunches. Beside him, Corker dug his hoofs in. The horses slid to a stop in a cloud of dust. They had brought up dead-end against a crisscrossed barrier of big spruce blow-downs, a tangle of upjutting branches and great masses of earth-caked roots. From beyond this barrier welled a frightful bellowing clamor.

Jed was off his horse. He jerked his rifle out of the boot and raced toward the blowdowns, shouting as he ran. Randy caught the word "blood." The rest was lost in the deafening uproar. The boy jumped to the ground, grabbed out his rifle, and sprinted after his father.

They clawed through the heavy limbs of the fallen trees. Branches lashed back at them. A broken limb snagged Jed's rifle. He brought a savage boot down, snapped the limb off. A big tree trunk blocked his way. He scrambled up on top, crawled forward along the trunk, worming his way around and over the branches.

Randy struggled after him. The boy's ears were ringing. A whole herd of cows was bellowing now. Rough bark bloodied the boy's hands and knees. He was panting. All at once he felt the tree trunk they were on shift sickeningly, teeter forward. He froze.

"Hold it!" his father shouted. "Don't budge." Jed laid his rifle down and reached out and parted the branches.

Randy caught his breath. The trunk they knelt on lay fallen out over a deep ravine, a good forty feet across and twenty deep. Randy gazed down at the yawning drop and shivered. Tall jagged boulders jutted up from the bottom of the ravine. The boy raised scared eyes. His breath caught. "Pa!" he stammered. "Over there! Look!"

Through the opening in the branches they stared out across the ravine. On the far side was a large clearing. In the center, not thirty feet beyond the ravine, a giant silvertip grizzly crouched facing a black longhorn bull. The grass around them was trampled.

The black bull stood quietly, head and tail high, burnished, uphooking horns gleaming. Randy shivered. The glossy black hide was caked with muck. Blood dripped from long gashes in one shoulder.

Jed gave a strangled cry. "It's my black bull!"

"Pa!" Randy cried. "Those bulls back there at the edge of the timber!"

They were massed back under the trees beyond

the grizzly and the black bull, a dozen or more great rangy bulls, high backs to the timber, wicked out-swept horns lowered. Angrily they pawed the earth, digging it up with their horns, their hoarse bellows rumbling higher and higher to shrill, grating screams.

"It's the blood call!" Jed choked. "They've smelled blood! They're crazy!"

He rose awkwardly to one knee, clinging to a branch as the tree trunk swayed sickeningly over the ravine. Cautiously he broke off twigs and branches until he had a clear sight. He brought his rifle up, steadying it across a limb.

"If you shoot, you'll hit the bull!" Randy cried.

"He'll move," his father said grimly. "I'll wait till I get the grizzly in the clear."

At that instant the black bull put his head down and charged. The grizzly awaited him, crouching. The bull's head hit with crashing thump against the grizzly's ribs. The bear went down. The bull's head tilted, wicked horns poised for the gore. Suddenly the bear's great shaggy head shot up. Yellowed fangs shut on the bull's nose. Huge forepaws came up and clamped the bull's neck.

The black bull went crazy. The great body humped. Murderous hoofs stomped the grizzly.

"They're killing each other!" Jed groaned.

"Pa!" Randy screamed. "The bulls! The bulls back there at timber!"

Heads to the ground, the bunched bulls were charging. Bellowing, plunging, they surged down upon the grizzly and the black bull.

"Shoot!" Jed shouted. "Over their heads! Shoot!"

The boy jerked his rifle up. Both rifles roared. They roared again and again. The seething mass of screaming, maddened animals panicked. Bulls and grizzly fled headlong into the timber. Slowly their wild bellows faded. Dust billowed and swirled in the empty clearing.

Shakily Randy lowered his empty rifle. He looked at his father. Jed knelt staring at the empty clearing. A muscle twitched along his jaw.

"Pa." Randy's voice trembled.

Slowly his father turned. "Let's get back off this tree, Randy. I want to get across and have a look at that clearing."

They backed awkwardly out through the tangle of branches while the tree swayed and teetered. When they were safely back from the ravine, they slid to the ground.

"Down this way," Jed nodded.

Randy followed his father as he scrambled over and around boulders and blowdowns along the bank of the ravine. At last Jed found a spot where the bank sloped enough to give them footing. He went down first.

"Mind your gun barrel," he yelled as he coasted to the bottom in caving dirt.

Randy followed him down in a slide of rocks and earth. They hurried across the ravine and clambered up over boulders and out into the clearing. Randy shivered at the bloody, hoof-pocked turf.

Bending over, Jed started slowly over the battle-field, scanning the trampled soil. "Looks like a hundred bulls cut up this ground, instead of a dozen," he grunted. "Circle out wide around the clearing, Randy. See if you can find which way the grizzly ran."

Randy obeyed. Slowly he walked along the edge of the timber, searching the loamy soil. His hands were sweaty against his rifle stock. He kept glancing nervously at the dark, silent timber.

In a stand of pine saplings on the far side of the clearing, he found the grizzly's tracks. The skin on the back of his neck prickled. The grizzly had not slowed for the stand of young pines, but had crashed headlong through them, leaving a trail of broken tree trunks.

Randy spun around. "They're over here, Pa!" he shouted. "Here's the grizzly's tracks!"

Jed crossed the clearing at a run. He followed the

grizzly's trail through the battered saplings for a dozen yards. Suddenly he stopped, knelt down.

Randy pushed his way through the pines to his father's side. Jed raised a grim face. "The silvertip's the grizzly that wrecked our cabin," he said flatly. "See, here's the track of that three-toed hind paw."

Randy stared down at the huge track of the crippled paw outlined in the duff. He licked dry lips. "What are we going to do, Pa?"

His father got to his feet. "If I did what I wanted," he said softly, "I'd round up the dogs and track that grizzly down."

"Are we going to?" Randy asked eagerly.

Jed shook his head. "We can't. Our life depends on the dogs. We couldn't ever build us up a herd without them. We can't risk losing even one. Besides, I swore when we came up here that I wasn't hunting grizzlies unless they did harm to us or our herd. I ain't changed my mind."

"But, Pa—"

"Look, Randy, you know a longhorn bull's just about the fiercest critter on four feet. You saw what that grizzly was doing to that bull, didn't you?"

Randy nodded, biting at his lip. "You know something, Pa?" he asked. "I can't ever remember being scared down home in the Brasada, but seeing that grizzly—he scared me."

"That ain't nothing to be ashamed of," Jed told him.

"It wasn't only he was so big and so fierce," the boy went on. "I think it was how fast he was on his feet. One minute he was there, about to kill that ferocious bull, and the next, he was gone. Like a spook. Disappeared."

"Spook," Jed repeated. "That's a good name for him."

"Reckon why him and the bull were fighting, Pa?"

"Likely as not the bunch of bulls panicked the bear. Don't forget we stampeded that bunch back down on the mountain. Likely they came crashing out of timber on him without warning, and he just went for the nearest bull."

The boy shivered.

"Randy," Jed said slowly, "I was thinking—there's no need to tell Ma about the grizzly fighting the bull. You understand why. I don't want to fret her about grizzlies more than's needful."

Randy nodded.

"Come on then, let's get for home. Night's coming on fast."

9 RANDY'S ELK

The moon stood high in the sky when Jed and Randy rode up the slope to the cabin. Light gleamed at the windows.

"Seems like a week since we brought in Mr. Sam's cow and calf this morning," Randy sighed. "Lordy, I'm hungry. Look, Pa, there's Mr. Sam watching for us at the window."

A rock turned under Pepper's hoof and he stumbled, whinnying. Up at the cabin, dogs barked.

"Well, at least the dogs came home," Jed grunted. "I bet the idiots chased those wild cows plumb out of the Big Horns. Randy, mind you don't forget we're not telling Ma about the grizzly fighting the black bull."

"No, sir, I won't forget."

The cabin door flung open. Mr. Sam stood silhouetted in lamplight, nightshirt flapping about bare feet.

"It's them!" he bellowed. "It's them!"

"Ho, Mr. Sam," Jed called. "Where's your Ma?"

Molly appeared in the doorway, drying her hands on her apron. "You boys all right?" she called anxiously.

Mr. Sam came down off the porch with a whoop. "The dogs've been home since sundown," he shouted. "Ma, she had to rub their paws with bear grease, they're that cut up. You catch any more wild cows, Pa, huh?"

"Whoa, fellow," his father grunted, swinging to the ground. "We left a couple of heifers and two cows tied up in the timber beyond Beaver Pond." He turned and looked up at his wife. "Molly girl, we found the vanished longhorns! Maybe you think we don't have a story to tell you."

"Jed! Not the vanished herd!"

"Not the whole herd, maybe, but a mountain valley swarming with wild cows. More'n enough for us to build up a real herd."

She came down off the porch. "I just can't believe it."

"Well, we did. Of course, there's still the business of catching them. Jumping Jehoshaphat, what a day! Dish up the vittles while we unsaddle, girl. We're about starved. We'll tell you all about the long-horns while we eat."

That was Monday night. Next day Jed and Randy made two trips with the neck oxen and brought down the wild cows tied above Beaver Pond.

"We starting out after longhorns in the morning?" Randy asked as they lounged before the fire that night.

Jed shook his head. "I've changed my plans. We're going to build a barn and corral close to the cabin, and a shed for wild hay. Soon as she weans her calf, I aim to make a milker out of the wild cow Mr. Sam rounded up for us."

Mr. Sam bounced up from where he lay sprawled on the floor. "You know what, Pa? Ma named my calf Prissy Britches, on account he's so feisty, and I named his mammy Mrs. Friendly Old Girl."

"That goring, kicking wildcat!" Jed said in a strangled voice. "You sure picked her a likely name, Mr. Sam."

For five days Jed and Randy felled pines. Molly and Mr. Sam snaked the logs down as fast as they were trimmed. By Saturday Jed decided they had enough.

Sunday morning the Martins rode over. They brought venison steaks to fry.

"I'm sorry it's not more," Sarah Martin apologized. "Our meat's about gone."

"Our meat's gone, too, and guess what?" Mr. Sam said excitedly. "Randy's going elk hunting tomorrow. I can't go till next year when I'm six, but Randy's going to give me the antlers."

"Can I go with Randy, Pa?" Hal asked eagerly.

Henry Martin hesitated.

"Randy'd be proud to have Hal along," Jed said.

"If they promise they won't go traipsing off after no grizzly—" Henry said hesitantly.

"There'll be no bear hunting," Jed assured him.

"I reckon then he can go," Henry said slowly. "Well, Jed, found any wild cow tracks yet?"

"A few. Got our first five wild cows gentling down in our trap pasture corral."

"What!"

"And Prissy Britches," Mr. Sam cried. "Don't forget him."

"And Prissy Britches," Jed nodded. "A bull calf, Henry. Belongs to the first wild cow we caught."

"Five cows and a calf the first week!" Henry exclaimed. "Man alive, Jed!"

"I can tell you something better'n that, Henry. Me and Randy found the mountain valley that's the wild herd's bedding ground. We're in business, Henry."

"My Lord, Jed," Henry cried, "why don't you ride down to Buffalo and hire riders and round up the whole herd at one time?"

Jed shook his head. "Couldn't afford to hire enough cowboys to hold that many wild cows. We'll just have to do it the brush popper's way—catch a few at a time. Hold them in the canyon corral till they get used to people and horses and dogs and we can turn them out with our Texas herd."

"Let's mosey down to your corral," Henry proposed. "I want a look at those wild cows."

"Sure. Mr. Sam, you stay here and play with Susie. Randy, you and Hal come along with us."

They walked around the cabin. "Say, what's all the logs for?" Henry asked.

"Barn and corral. Hay shed, too. We've got miles of wild hay, free for the cutting."

"Cowmen don't feed up here, Jed. They let stock drift and forage. Come spring, they all pitch in for a roundup and cut out their stuff."

"Turning your herd out to forage is all right for you fellows with big spreads, Henry. Me, I can't risk turning out wild cows that've just had my brand slapped on them. No, this winter I'll feed."

They were almost down to the canyon corral when Jed stopped. "Let's sit down on that log over there for a minute. Me and Randy have got something to tell you, something I didn't want the wives and the young'uns to hear."

When they were seated, Henry asked curiously: "Well, Jed?"

"First off, Henry, about a week ago me and Randy came across the tracks of a sow grizzly and a cub. It was in a clearing high up on the divide between Lobo and Baldy. The sow had been feeding on the carcass of a mule deer buck."

"Did you see her?" Hal asked eagerly.

Jed shook his head. "But farther on up in the timber we did see a grizzly," he said slowly, "a big silvertip male. It was like this—"

When he was finished, Henry let out a soft whistle. "You're sure, Jed, it was the same grizzly what tore up your cabin?"

"Sure. We found his tracks."

"What'll you do? I mean, if he's ranging between here and the wild longhorn herd—"

"We'll go right on catching wild cows," Jed said simply. "Like I said a while ago, Henry, I don't figure Spook for a cattle killer. It's my guess he was fighting that bull because they'd scared him. Just to be on the safe side, though, I aim to try to find out Spook's range, and if I'm lucky, where he dens up."

Henry shook his head slowly. "Well, all I've got to say is you've got more guts than I have."

"Ain't a matter of guts, Henry. I didn't come up here blind. I knew this was grizzly country. Having trouble with Spook is a chance we've got to take."

When the Martins went home that evening, they left Hal behind. He and Randy were in the saddle by dawn next morning. Jed came out as they were ready to set off.

"Which way you fellows aiming to ride?" he asked.

"I figured up Eagle Mountain," Randy told him. "I'd like to see where Grizzly Creek heads up."

"Good idea. Remember, Randy, no chasing after a grizzly."

"We promise, Pa. Look for us back around dark."

The horses were fresh and eager. They covered the canyon at a good clip. At the foot of Eagle,

Randy led the way up through open timber that bordered the tumbling mountain stream. The roar of the water drowned out the clatter of the horses' hoofs on the rocks.

The horses took the mountain slowly, climbing now through dense stands of spruce and pine, now through bunch grass parks and willowy meadows. Elk sign was abundant—saplings battered by bulls polishing horns, droppings, deep cleft hoof cuts in soft pockets of earth.

After a mile they forded the creek and rode across a wide park into timber. The air was thin and cold in the shadows. Red squirrels darted across the trail. Whisky-jacks scolded from trees.

They topped out over a shoulder and down into a narrow glade. All at once there came a flurry from the brush beside the stream, a loud crashing and snorting. A small herd of bull elk burst out into the open, quartering up toward timber in a wedge-shaped band, sailing gracefully over windfalls, noses high, antlers laid back.

Randy and Hal jerked rifles from saddle boots. The elk had disappeared into timber. Randy jabbed Pepper with his spurs. The roan stallion leaped out across the park. Ahead Randy caught a glimpse of the herd, moving in a fast, swinging trot single file down a twisting trail.

Pepper sailed over windfalls, skidded around turns, streaked down and up out of rocky ravines. Then the trail suddenly angled down the mountain, skirted an aspen flat, and continued along the brushy bank of Grizzly Creek. Randy took one quick look back. He had lost Hal.

Suddenly ahead in the timber the boy caught a glimpse of the creamy rump-patch of a feeding elk. His heart thudded. He reined up and slid to the ground. Licking his finger, he held it up. The wind was with him. He tied Pepper to an aspen, then glided down the trail.

He could see the herd through the trees. They were scattered out over a grassy park flanked by a steep, aspen-clad slope. As they fed they raised nervous heads, watching their back trail.

Randy left the trail and eased through a tangle of windfalls to the shelter of a big boulder on the edge of the park where the grassland joined the meandering border of aspen. His eyes were on a big black-necked, light-sided buck feeding a little apart from the rest. Randy brought his rifle up, steadying it across the boulder. He sighted, aiming for a neck shot. Slowly his finger tightened on the trigger.

At that instant there came a loud crashing from back in the timber, a noisy shout. "Randy! Randy!"

The elk panicked. They leaped away in a run,

necks thrust out, antlers back. For a second Randy had a good quartering shot at the buck. His rifle roared. The buck staggered. Again the rifle roared. The buck went down, fell on his side. The herd vanished into the timber.

At that moment Hal's buckskin burst out into the park. Hal reined him back on his haunches. "Golly, Randy," Hal said contritely, "I nearly spoiled your shot."

"You sure spooked them," Randy said flatly. "Lucky Pa's not along. You'd get it."

"And I know better," Hal admitted glumly. "When I lost you back there, I got spooked myself. Reckon I've been hearing too much about grizzlies."

Randy levered a cartridge into the chamber of his rifle and started down the slope. "Let's bleed him out."

The buck had fallen with his head downslope at the foot of a huge twisted pine. Randy felt a quick surge of joy when he gazed down at the heavy-beamed antlers, six points on each side, a spread of four feet. The tines still wore shreds of velvet.

"Golly, but he's a beauty," Hal said admiringly. "Have you killed a lot of elk, Randy?"

"Ain't killed any before," Randy told him, reaching for the bowie knife at his belt. "Ain't never seen one before. I knew what they were because of the antlers Pa nailed over the porch steps at the cabin. Let's get at it, Hal. We've still got to get you an elk."

They gutted the buck, propping open the split brisket and pelvis with sticks. "We'll string him up in the pine out of reach of varmints and pack him out in the morning," Randy told Hal. "Pitch me your lariat."

They stretched the rope flat and rolled the carcass on top of it. Randy knotted the rope tight up under the forelegs. Then he tossed the end of the rope through the crotch in the pine. Hal caught it, tied it to his saddle horn. He mounted Buck and backed him away until the carcass swung clear.

"Hold it!" Randy shouted when the long hind legs dangled three feet off the ground. "Circle the tree. Whoa, that'll do it. Give me the end of the rope."

Quickly he tied the rope, then stepped back and studied the dangling carcass. "That'll hold him," he said with satisfaction. "Fetch Pepper, Hal, while I wash up in the creek."

10 GRIZZLY WATERFALL

Back in the saddle, Randy swung Pepper east up the bank of the creek. "When I shot my elk, the herd ran this way," he told Hal. "They won't run far."

On their right was the steep pine-clad mountain slope, broken by cliffs. On their left Grizzly Creek had narrowed into a noisy torrent of white water that boiled down around weathered boulders.

They were climbing. The trail followed high above the twisting course of the creek in its narrow rocky gorge. Stunted pines clung to the sides of the gorge, their tips dipping and swaying just under the trail.

For a quarter of a mile the horses toiled up around boulders and windfalls. Suddenly the trail bent sharply to the right around an outjutting cliff. Beyond, a stacked-up jumble of fallen boulders blocked their path. The boys swung the horses to the right up into timber, circling the boulders as closely as they could.

From behind the piled-up rocks came the dull roar of the creek. The wind knifed down cold. Overhead the sun filtered down feebly through the canopy of pine boughs.

The timber thinned as they climbed. Brush grew thick between the trees. They rode at last upon an undergrowth without opening, and reined up.

"Reckon we've lost the elk," Hal said gloomily.

"Don't give up so easy, Hal. Let's give the horses a breather and scout around for a way through the brush."

They tied the horses to pines and took their rifles. They plodded up along the wall of brush, boot heels digging into soft turf. Whisky-jacks followed them, fluttering from tree to tree with raucous cries.

Striped chipmunks scurried along logs. A sleepy marmot roused from the top of a sunlit rock, whistled in alarm, then disappeared beneath a ledge.

The boys trudged around a curve. All at once there was the light drumming of hoofs. A mule deer doe streaked out of the timber, crossed in front of them, and vanished into the brush fifty yards ahead.

"See that?" Randy cried. "Must be a game trail up there!" He broke into a run.

He found the game trail, a wide trail tunneling away into the high brush. His heart pounded as he stared down at tracks big as platters sunk deep in the hard-packed earth.

"It's a grizzly trail," he panted as Hal raced up.

The trail was an old one. The huge tracks were at least twelve inches long.

"Golly!" Hal gasped.

Randy thumbed back the hammer of his rifle.

"What are you aiming to do?" Hal asked nervously.

"Follow the trail. What's the matter, you scared?"

"Reckon I am, a little," Hal said honestly. "Remember, I told you I never had done much hunting, and that just with Pa. Besides, I've got to get me an elk, Randy. We need meat."

"That doe took this trail. Likely your elk did, too. Anyway, you know Pa said he wanted us to learn the bear trails around here. Come on."

Breathlessly they followed the huge sunken tracks through the brush and out into timber beyond. In a clump of pines they came upon a large oval depression, a foot deep, lined with thick layers of pine needles.

"I'll bet anything it's a grizzly's laying-up bed," Randy said excitedly. "Ben Waters told Pa grizzlies dig beds like this along trails for napping. Come on."

Hal followed him around the laying-up bed and back onto the bear trail. "We must be getting back to the creek, Randy," he said. "I can hear water roaring."

Randy cocked his ear. "By golly, you're right. Sounds like we're right on it."

They followed the trail as it meandered through the trees. Suddenly they emerged from the timber into a wide clearing. Straight across from them a towering wall of weathered granite curved toward the northeast. The wall was split by a deep V-shaped gorge. Beyond the split they could see where the gorge cut deep into the mountain. The floor of the gorge climbed steeply up toward the pine-clad ridge below the granite summit of Eagle Mountain.

"Look at the boulders and windfalls stacked up in that gorge," Hal cried. "Looks like a Kansas tornado hit it!"

Randy grinned. "This is the Big Horns. Snow melts in the spring and starts avalanches. That's what cut that gorge up there and brought down the rocks and trees."

At that moment a sudden gust of cold wind whipped down through the split. Sand stung the boys' faces.

"Let's go back," Hal shivered. "We're not going to find any elk around here."

"Don't go balky now, Hal. This bear trails heads through that split. I bet you anything the gorge leads straight up to the creek. Listen to her roar. Can't be more'n a couple hundred feet up."

They followed the trail as it wound in and around boulders and windfalls toward the gap in the wall. As they clambered over loose rock and waded through drifts of gravel, they studied the steep climb ahead. All at once, Randy stopped.

"Look!" He was pointing toward the pine spirals atop the highest ridge. "Look, an eagle!"

The huge bird was soaring in wide circles, wings outspread. Suddenly the bird braked, hung poised for a moment, wings pumping, then swooped down and disappeared behind the pine tops.

"Reckon it's got a nest up there?" Hal asked.

Randy shook his head. "Not near high or rocky enough."

"You aim to climb clean up there?"

"I—Look, Hal, the eagle's back. He's got a fish in his claws. The creek's back of the pines, all right. Come on, hurry."

They followed the winding grizzly trail through the split and into the gorge. There Hal stopped.

"It's crazy for us to try to climb up over those trees and big rocks just to see where this bear trail leads," he fumed. "Let's turn back."

Randy shook his head stubbornly. "Not after we've come this far. Look at the grizzly tracks, Hal. Worn so deep they're good as steps in the rocks. Come on."

They scrambled up over a tumbled maze of granite boulders. They crawled under toppled tree trunks. They crunched up, up over sliding rock. They brought up at last under a jumble of tangled blowdowns.

"I don't like this place," Hal panted. "It's spooky."

'We can't stop here," Randy gasped.

They pushed ahead, hauling themselves up over blowdowns, scrabbling for handholds on rock. The roar of the creek grew louder. The trail swung sharp to the left. Panting, the boys struggled around outjutting rocks. Ahead, the trail led through a tunnel formed by huge fallen rock slabs.

"Golly, but it's dark in there," Hal gasped.

"We're almost there," said Randy tensely. "Listen to the creek roar. You got your gun on ready?"

"I got it," Hal said nervously.

"I'll go first. Give me a little room." Randy stooped and led the way into the tunnel. It was dark inside. The fetid stink of bear burned his nostrils. He felt his way along the wall with his gun barrel. All at once the barrel hit solid rock.

"Sharp turn," he warned Hal, who was stumbling along close behind.

They eased around. Beyond, the tunnel widened. There was the glimmer of daylight ahead. The roar of the rushing creek reverberated from rock walls.

"Watch for that low ceiling," Randy warned. "We best crawl the rest of the way."

Awkwardly they crawled toward the sunlit opening. They reached it, and stopped, blinking at dazzling sunlight.

"Holy jumped-up Moses!" Hal breathed.

Less than twenty yards across from them they could see, through a rainbow of mist and spray, a terrifying sheet of white water blasting down through a bed of jutting rocks, plunging, tumbling, shooting over the brink of a cliff, hurtling down a sheer granite wall toward a gorge far below.

The boys stared, breathless. Randy ran his tongue over dry lips. He was trembling.

Suddenly Hal grabbed his arm, pointing toward the torrent. A splintered tree trunk came floating down fast toward the brink. The huge trunk bucked and pitched, bobbed violently, then shot out over cascading white water.

Randy leaped to his feet. "Let's see where it lands!"

They hurried, clambering down over rocky ledges. They brought up on an overhanging shelf just below the fall. Dropping to hands and knees, they crawled out to the edge. Randy grasped the rim with both hands. He braced himself on his arms and leaned forward cautiously, peering over. He sucked in his breath. The shelf they crouched on hung out over a sheer precipice. A hundred feet below was a seething whirlpool of green-white water.

Breathlessly the boys watched as the tree trunk spun crazily in the whirlpool for a moment, then went under the bubbly gobs of the eddy's foam.

"See how it sucked that big trunk under!" Hal cried.

The din of the waterfall was deafening. Cold wind cut down through the gorge. The boys were drenched with spray.

Finally Hal pushed back from the edge. "Ready to go?" he asked. "That spray's too doggone cold."

Randy nodded. They clambered back over the

rocks to the bear trail. The tracks led up to the bank of the creek just above the fall. Here the water rushed between a scattering of big rock slabs. Randy gazed at the slabs. They jutted up above the white water all the way across to the timbered bank beyond the creek.

"I bet bears cross over on those slabs, Hal. They're like a bridge. Want to try it?"

"Not me." Hal plumped down on the bank. "You go right along. I aim to rest a spell."

Carefully Randy stepped over the foaming side water to the first slab. The flat rock stood a foot out of the current. It was wet with spray. With a long step Randy reached the next slab, then the next, and the next. He hesitated before the next slab. It was barely above water line. A wave washed over his boots as he stepped onto it.

Jumping from rock to rock, he reached the opposite bank. As his feet hit ground, he froze. Between the creek and the forest of tall pines was a narrow white beach. In the wet sand at the edge of the water were the bunched tracks of a grizzly.

Randy squatted down. Just above waterline were the prints of huge forepaws. Three inches in front of the pad marks were the long imprints of curved claws. The boy shivered. Water was oozing slowly into the tracks.

Randy got up. His glance swept the shadowy forest of pines uneasily. He turned and looked back across the creek. "Hal!" he hollered. "Fresh tracks! Come here!"

That brought Hal. He came hopping across from slab to slab.

"Hurry," Randy urged. "You can even see the creases on the soles of his pads, but they're filling up fast."

Hal reached the bank. His eyes widened. "Gosh!" he panted. "Gosh!"

"See?" Randy turned away toward the trees, pointing. "See, he came down out of the timber. You can see his tracks—" he broke off, staring at the ground.

"What's the matter?" Hal asked.

Randy knelt down. In the spongy soil was the imprint of a huge hind paw. The boy swallowed hard, looked up at Hal. "It's Spook's tracks. Look, here's the left hind paw mark. Two toes missing. Spook stood right there where you're standing and had himself a drink. Maybe he was watching us while we were watching that tree trunk go over the fall."

Hal stepped back, glanced about. "You ain't figuring on trailing him?" he asked uneasily.

"After we promised?"

"Pa's liable to whale me once he finds out we

even followed along a grizzly trail," Hal said unhappily.

"Not when we tell him and Pa what we found.
Now we know where Spook ranges. Now we can track
him down."

11 BEAR ON A LOG

The sun hung low over Elk Mountain when Randy and Hal rode back down into Bear Claw Canyon.

"Home before sundown," Randy said with satisfaction, "and an elk buck cooling up on the mountain."

"You got one," Hal grumbled. "Not me."

"We'll go halves on it, Hal. Finding Spook's range

was more important than getting another elk. Pa'll tell you so too, you'll see."

They rode slowly along Grizzly Creek, following a narrow cowpath that wound through dense stands of alders and mountain willows. On both sides of the trail, the ground was matted with blueberry bushes.

"Look," Randy pointed, "the berries are starting to turn. Ma aims to put up enough to last the winter."

Hal gazed hungrily at the tangle of low branched bushes with their clusters of scarlet berries. "I'm that hungry I could eat 'em green. But I'm proud we don't have any close to our cabin. Every bear in the territory will be down here when they get ripe."

Randy grinned. "There's plenty berries up on the mountains—" he broke off, cocking his ear. "Listen. I could swear I heard a horse neigh. Sounded like Poca."

They both heard it then, an outdrawn, frightened neighing that rose higher and higher until it broke off in a panicked squeal.

"That's Poca," Randy muttered. "She's in trouble."

He raked Pepper with his spurs. The roan stallion leaped forward. Hal's buckskin thundered on his heels. Randy swung Pepper sharply to the right. The horses burst out of the brush into open pasture.

The boys spotted Poca at the same instant. The paint came tearing out of the brush a hundred yards up the canyon and headed west toward the cabin at a gallop, saddle empty, stirrups flopping.

Randy reined Pepper back on his haunches. Hal pulled Buck to a sliding stop. "Reckon she pitched Mr. Sam off?"

"Not Mr. Sam," Randy said shortly, "but something sure as heck's wrong. Mr. Sam must be up there around the bend. Come on."

They sent their horses at a run up canyon. Swiftly Pepper drew away from the buckskin, leaving him far behind as he tore around the bend. Randy swung the stallion wide around a half-rotted blowdown, squinting against the glare of sunlight on water. Up by a clump of alders a giant windfallen cottonwood trunk lay halfway out across the creek. A big black bear stood on the trunk, facing the creek. Randy's heart lurched. Out at the very end of the trunk, just out of reach of the churning white water, Mr. Sam was crouched, face turned toward the bear.

Randy reined Pepper to a sliding stop. He leaped to the ground. Snatching his rifle out of the boot, he sprinted toward the toppled tree. He thumbed back the hammer as he ran. He saw the bear take one forward step.

"Please, God, don't let Mr. Sam move," he groaned.

But Mr. Sam was scrambling to his feet. He stood facing the bear, balancing awkwardly with outstretched arms. One hand still clutched a fishing pole. From the other dangled a string of fish.

"Throw him the fish!" Randy screamed as he ran.

At that instant Mr. Sam took one step toward the bear. He drew back the hand with the fish and swung. The fish whacked the bear squarely across the snout.

The bear half rose on its haunches, grabbed for the fish with both forepaws, missed. It slipped, teetered, clawing frantically at the log, then fell with a splash into the churning water.

Mr. Sam stood glaring down at the spot where the bear had gone under. His face with livid with fury. Just then the bear's black head broke the surface.

"You thieving varmint!" Mr. Sam bellowed. He raised his fishing pole and brought it down hard across the bear's head. "Take that," he roared, "and that, and that," and he brought the pole down again and again across the big black snout.

The bear half reared up out of the water. It raised both forepaws to protect its face from the rain of blows. Beady black eyes glared; black lips snarled back over yellowed teeth. A furious roar split the air.

Randy was on the log. Behind him he heard Hal's buckskin thunder up. He felt the log tremble as Hal hurried out toward him. He did not turn. The bear's beady eyes were on him now. The big jaws popped shut. Then with a growl the bear lunged for the log. Randy fired, the rifle barrel inches from the big black head. The bullet caught the bear between the eyes. The bear slumped into the water. Crimson foam stained the surface.

"You all right, Mr. Sam?" Randy panted.

"No, I ain't all right!" Mr. Sam roared. "That confounded varmint got my fish!"

Randy's knees went weak. He sat down hard on the log and stared at his little brother.

"He didn't get your fish, Mr. Sam," Hal said. Kneeling down he fumbled alongside the log, then held up the string of fish. "Stringer snagged on a limb."

From the slope above came the pound of hoofs, the barking of dogs. The boys turned, just as Jed flung himself off Poca. "What in tarnation—" he demanded, then broke off as the leopard dogs splashed out into the water to where the carcass of the bear had rolled with the current into the shallows beside a low boulder.

"You got to leave me tote my rifle, Pa," Mr. Sam said aggrievedly. "That old bear got me cornered out here on the log. Hadn't been for Randy, he'd of ate my fish for sure, and maybe he'd of ate me, too."

His father swallowed hard. He gazed at the carcass. Its gleaming black fur lifted and spread on the water.

"When Poca galloped in without Mr. Sam—" Jed began, then broke off, shaking his head. "I don't know if I ought to be proud or sorry he ain't afeared of nothing," he confided to Randy and Hal. "You know, fellows, the Lord sure works in funny ways. Just this morning Ma was counting over the reasons I needed to get a black bear—meat for the dogs, grease for making soap, cooking grease, grease for doctoring—"

"Pa," Randy interrupted, "what's got into the dogs?"

The leopard dogs had come splashing up out of the creek, were racing away up the slope, noses to the ground. They headed straight for a gnarled and twisted pine a hundred feet upslope. They swarmed around the trunk, noses high, excited barks splitting the air.

"They're barking treed," Jed said surprisedly. "You don't reckon there's another—" He started up the slope at a run.

The boys scrambled to the bank and raced after

him, Mr. Sam far in the rear. Under the tree Jed pushed the dogs aside. He peered up through the twisted branches.

"By golly, there's a cub up there!" he exclaimed as Randy and Hal ran up. "Mr. Sam's bear was a sow. She's put her cub up the pine. See, out there on that forked limb."

Mr. Sam came puffing up. He squirmed in beside his father. "Lemme see," he panted, "lemme see."

"On that forked limb," his father pointed. "See?"

"Yup," Mr. Sam panted, "and I see another one, too. Way up there in that crotch at the top of the tree."

"By golly, he's right," Jed exclaimed.

"We going to shoot them?" Hal asked excitedly.

"No, we ain't gonna shoot 'em!" Mr. Sam bellowed. "They're mine! I'm gonna catch 'em! They're mine!"

Jed looked down at the eager little face. "Reckon in a way you've got them coming to you," he said slowly, "on account of how you faced up to their mammy. But I don't rightly know how your Ma'll cotton to you making pets out of a couple of bear cubs."

"Ma won't mind," Mr. Sam said stoutly. "Gimme a heist up the tree, Pa. I want to catch my cubs."

"Whoa, fellow," his father grinned, "catching

cubs ain't all that easy. Randy, you hightail it up to the cabin and fetch down a couple of gunny sacks. Take the dogs with you and leave them. Hal, you go get me the rope off Poca's saddle horn."

"What do you want me to do?" Mr. Sam asked eagerly.

"Just you stay back out of the way, fellow. Your Pa's likely to have his hands full with those little cusses."

When the boys returned with the sacks and rope, Jed made a loop in the lariat and draped the rope around his neck. Then he went up the tree.

The cub on the forked limb started backing away. As Jed climbed up even with the limb, the cub reached the end. He clung there coughing and woofing. Jed hooked one leg around the tree trunk, bracing himself against a limb, then eased the lariat from around his neck. He shook out the loop and threw. The cub struck the rope away with one paw. Jed threw again. The rope circled the cub's fat neck. Before Jed could jerk it tight, the cub had it off. Jed straightened the loop and threw. The noose caught. Jed jerked it tight.

The cub put up a struggle, biting, clawing, snorting. Suddenly he slipped on the swaying limb, lost his footing, tumbled off, and dangled in the air. The sudden weight on the rope almost jerked Jed from his perch. Quickly he played out the rope. "Watch those claws," he called to the boys.

The cub was still fighting. The fat black body twisted and squirmed at the end of the rope. Razor-sharp claws slashed out. But the cub's breath was going fast. Suddenly he gave up, hung limp. Hal grabbed the rope and held it steady, while Randy maneuvered the cub into a sack. Hal slipped off the noose. Randy tied the sack tight. The frightened cub lay still inside the sack.

Jed pulled the rope up and climbed higher. The second cub was smaller. Its pointed little snout poked at him around the tree trunk. A thin little voice woofed.

"Not much ginger in you," said Jed, grinning.

The next time jet-black eyes peeked at him around the trunk, he tossed the loop. It settled over the black head. Jed jerked it tight and slowly pulled the cub out of the crotch. The shiny black body hung limp, little forepaws doubled against the chest.

Carefully Jed lowered the cub. "Easy on this one," he cautioned. "She's already scared half to death."

While the boys got the second cub into a sack, Jed clambered down. He brushed at the pine needles sticking to his levis.

"Well, Mr. Sam, I hope you're satisfied," he grunted. "From now on those cubs are up to you."

12 SPOOK TURNS BANDIT

Randy came awake. Dawn showed gray at the window. His mother and father were still asleep in their bunk bed. Hal lay wrapped in a buffalo robe in front of the fireplace.

Seeing him there brought back the excitement of the day before. Randy grinned. His mother had not been happy about the cubs. She had told Mr. Sam that he could not keep them in the cabin. It had ended with Randy and Hal lopping off the limbs of a big pine blowdown above the cabin and building a stout cage. Mr. Sam had been underfoot the entire time, keeping the dogs away from the squirming gunny sacks. To the dogs, bear smell was bear smell. They could not understand that the cubs were not to be touched.

Randy turned over on his back and stretched lazily. Beside him Mr. Sam lay curled up in a knot, one fist tucked under his cheek. Randy smiled. Mr. Sam had stayed beside the cage until long after dark, patiently trying to coax the frightened cubs to a pan of milk. They would have none of it or of him. They cowered, terrified, as far away as they could get, woofing and growling when he thrust his hand through the bars. Mr. Sam was tearfully certain that the cubs would starve before morning.

Randy reached out and patted the little fellow's rump gently. Mr. Sam was a good one.

It wouldn't do any harm just to see if the cubs were all right. Pushing back the quilt, he slid out of the bunk. The floor was cold to his bare feet. Noiselessly he gathered up clothes and boots and tiptoed to the door, easing outside. He shivered in his long underwear. As he pulled on levis and shirt, he gazed out across the canyon. Swirls of gray mist lifted on the breeze. Down along Grizzly Creek the longhorns grazed peacefully, high sharp backs standing tall out of the grass. The longhorns had taken to the canyon pasture. They were packing on tallow.

He sat down on the step and tugged on his boots. Behind him the cabin door squeaked. He turned just as Mr. Sam slipped out, clothes tucked under his arm.

"You seen my cubs?" the little boy demanded. "They all right?"

"Ain't been out back yet. Get dressed. I'll wait."

Mr. Sam clapped his old hand-me-down Stetson on his head, skinned into levis and shirt, stamped his feet into his boots. "Brrr, but it's cold. Come on, I'm ready."

As the boys rounded the cabin the black cubs backed away into a corner of the cage, cowering close together. Mr. Sam squatted down and peered through the bars. "Their pan's upside down," he wailed, "and all the milk's spilt."

Randy knelt down beside him. "They drank it, Mr. Sam. They've just been playing with the pan."

"You reckon?" Mr. Sam stuck his hand through the bars. "Here, cubby, cubby," he wheedled, "come to Mr. Sam."

The bigger cub growled, baring sharp little teeth. He struck out at Mr. Sam's hand. Mr. Sam jerked back.

"Careful there," Randy cautioned, "those claws are like needles."

"I'm going up to the cabin, Randy, and snitch a can of milk for their breakfast."

"Wait. What'd you do with your fish last night?"

"Gutted 'em and put 'em in a pail of water."

"Fetch me one. Cubs like fish."

Mr. Sam scurried up to the cabin. He brought back a fat speckled trout. With his bowie knife Randy cut it into small chunks. The cubs had caught the smell. They watched, beady-eyed, pointed black snouts working.

"Now feed them a piece at a time," Randy directed. "Take it slow. Don't scare them."

Carefully Mr. Sam dropped a piece in front of each cub. They pounced with little woofs, then waited for more, black eyes glittering.

Randy got up. "Talk to them, Mr. Sam. They're just babies, and they're lonesome for their mammy."

"You stay and help me, Randy."

Randy shook his head. "Time to rout the folks out. We've got to go back up on Eagle and pack out my elk."

There were flapjacks for breakfast, golden brown outside, the inside streaked with blue from the Indian meal they had bought on the trail up. And there was side meat, sizzling hot from the skillet, and honey, and steaming black coffee.

"It's a real pretty day," Molly sighed. "I'll be proud when you boys can take it easier."

Her husband pushed back from the table. "First things first, Molly. We've got to fetch down Randy's elk and dress it out. And then the black bear. We just gutted it and strung it up to a cottonwood last night. And I want to wean Prissy Britches, soon's we get the barn built here at the cabin and get Mrs. Friendly Old Girl up here away from the rest of the wild cows."

"Pretty soon we'll need the bear grease, too. I'll render it in the morning."

Jed got to his feet. "You boys ready to saddle up?"

Half an hour later Jed and Randy and Hal rode east down the canyon, Jed leading Poca, the leopard dogs trailing the horses.

Fog clouds hugged the timbered slopes of Eagle Mountain. Above them its craggy crest jutted out as though suspended in mid-air. As the sun climbed above the mountain, the clouds lifted and dissipated. The granite crags loomed starkly white in the sunlight.

The horses took the first slope at a brisk walk. They followed the twisting course of the stream as it churned down over the rocks. Squirrels scampered across the trail. The east wind blew cold through the timber.

As they climbed higher, Jed studied the elk sign with satisfaction. "One thing for sure," he told the boys, "we won't lack for meat."

"What about old Spook?" Hal asked uneasily.

Jed's face sobered. "Like I told your Pa the other day, Hal, I don't figure we've got real cause to worry about that grizzly. I'll have to admit I do feel a mite better now, knowing where he ranges. I'm proud you two followed his trail yesterday."

"Randy said you'd want us to," Hal said.

"You boys did the right thing. How much farther to that elk of yours, Randy?"

"About a quarter of a mile, maybe less."

The trail steepened. Wind whistled down through the timber. The horses were sweating. In the cold air their breath puffed out in gray streamers. Nobody talked much. All three rode with heads tucked against the wind.

They topped out over a high shoulder into the narrow glade where the boys had ridden upon the elk herd.

"Here's where we spooked the herd," Randy told his father. "Won't be far now."

He led the way along the winding trail through the timber. When the trail angled down the mountain to the bank of Grizzly Creek, Randy looked back. "The park's dead ahead, Pa," he called over the roar of the water. "See, here it is. There's the pine where he's strung up. There—" his voice trailed off. He reined up short. He sat staring open-mouthed.

"What's wrong?" Jed asked. "What's got into you?"

Randy's lips moved. No sound came. He cleared his throat. "My elk's gone," he said huskily.

He spurred Pepper and the roan stallion plunged out across the park. Then all at once the leopard dogs cut loose. With a blast of wild barks they streaked past the stallion. They raced straight for the pine.

Randy reined Pepper back on his haunches beside the tree. The dogs were milling excitedly, noses rooting the ground. Ten feet above, the frayed end of the lariat swayed gently in the wind.

Randy swung to the ground as Jed and Hal galloped up. He pushed the dogs aside. His eyes swept the ground. "It was a bear," he said. "The dogs have rooted his tracks so, I can't rightly—Pa, it was a grizzly! It—" he broke off, knelt down. Close up to the trunk the huge tracks were sunk deep in loamy soil, the long claw marks showing plainly out in front. Randy plucked a small patch of elk hide out of one track. He got to his feet, fingering the scrap of hide, his brown eyes blazing.

"It was Spook, Pa. See, there by that root, the track with the three-toed back paw? Spook stole the very first elk I ever killed!"

Jed dismounted and walked over to the boy. "That evil so-and-so," he swore softly. "Pulled your elk out of the pine, then laid down and stuffed his belly right here. There's the print of his whole ornery carcass."

"Mr. Reynolds," Hal cried, "look at the dogs."

The three spotted dogs were across the park and on the timbered slope that rose to the south.

"They've picked up Spook's trail," Randy cried.

"You can read the tracks yourself," Jed told him. "See here, where they bear down deep? Spook picked up the carcass right here—not clean up—must have grabbed it by the neck. See the thin line on each side the drag marks? That's where the elk's hind hoofs dragged the ground. Let's follow the dogs. They'll lead us where the blamed bandit stashed the carcass."

They followed the dogs on foot up into timber, in and around the boulders that scattered the steep slope. Jed walked with his rifle on ready. He stopped for a moment beside a big blowdown, pointing. The bear had climbed over. The rotted wood showed splintered gashes of claws, showed splotches, dried and brown.

Close beside a spruce the dogs were milling around a heap of dry branches and logs.

"We'll find what's left of your elk under that trash," Jed told Randy.

"There's the antlers sticking out," Hal pointed.

"See, Pa, a six-pointer, just like I told you," Randy said unhappily.

"Give me a hand, fellows," Jed told them.

They fell upon logs and branches, tugging them away. They uncovered the carcass. The grizzly had ripped a fore-quarter from the elk.

Jed stooped and studied the ragged shoulder. He brushed away green flies that clung to the flesh. "Torn off this morning," he muttered. "That thieving varmint's bedded down somewhere in the timber, sleeping it off."

"We could track him down with the dogs, Pa."

Jed shook his head. "Not with our dogs, we can't. And besides, don't forget Ma's waiting for us to skin the black bear. You fellows give me a hand with the carcass. There's still meat aplenty for both families. And Hal, that question you asked me coming up—I don't know, now. Spook tore up our cabin. He tried to kill the black bull I want. Now, this. I just don't know."

13 CATTLE KILLER

Along the banks of Grizzly Creek, ripening berries hung in thick clusters on the bushes. On the foothill slopes aspen slowly tinged with gold. At night the wind howled down cold out of the northwest, but the days were warm and sunny in Bear Claw Canyon. It was September.

The Reynolds herd was growing. The four wild

cows that Jed and Randy had first caught grazed peacefully now out in the Texas herd. The neck oxen had beaten a wide trail straight down the mountain from Vanished Longhorn Meadow and out across Bear Claw Canyon to the Little Brasada. Twelve wild cows and five wild steers were gentling down in the canyon corral.

Thirty yards behind the cabin, Jed and Randy had built a log barn and shed inside a corral with a high log fence. They had moved Mrs. Friendly Old Girl and Prissy Britches up to the barn. The bull calf had been weaned. Jed was slowly gentling Mrs. Friendly Old Girl down into a milker.

Jed and Randy were honed down to hard muscle. Day after day they labored from dawn to dusk, hunting wild cows, cutting wood against the coming winter, scything and spreading hay in side canyons. They would drag in dead tired at dark, dozing off at the supper table before Molly had cleared away the dishes.

"I'll be proud when the snows come and you can rest up a little," she told them one evening as they slumped yawning over supper. "Mr. Sam, get away from that door. You're not feeding the cubs inside tonight."

"Aw, Ma." Mr. Sam went to her, cuddled up against her, patted her arm. "Just till they eat, Ma, huh?" he wheedled, cutting his eyes up at her.

"Oh, I reckon you might as well," she gave in, rumpling his yellow curls, "but mind you make them behave."

Mr. Sam raced to the door and swung it wide. Two black furry balls catapulted into the cabin, skidding to a stop beside the pan of scraps Molly set on the floor. Black snouts rooted in the pan. Black rumps wiggled ecstatically.

"I warned Mr. Sam, today, if those cubs tear up one thing more around the cabin, we're getting rid of them," Molly told her husband.

"You sure called them right, when you named them Topsy and Turvy," Jed grinned. "Well, Mr. Sam, let's get them out in their cage. It's time we all got to bed. Sunup'll be here before we know it."

Randy followed them outside. Topsy and Turvy raced up the porch to where the leopard dogs lay curled against the wall. The cubs scrambled in among them, woofing and growling, wanting to play. The dogs ignored them. Pard got up and padded down to Randy, crowding against the boy's legs, whining. Randy sat down on the step and hugged Pard to him. "The canyon's pretty in the moon-light," he said dreamily.

Silvery light from a full moon flooded the canyon, silhouetting black shapes of cows in high grass, sparkling the churning water of Grizzly Creek. The granite peaks of the mountain chain towered ghostly white against the darkness of the sky. From the mountain above the cabin came the lonesome, drawn-out howl of a timber wolf. Randy felt Pard stiffen. The dog pulled away from him. Then from across the canyon came an answering howl, high, mournful, rising, falling, dying away. Pard's scruff bristled.

"There's the wilderness for you," Jed sighed softly. "Our canyon here, peaceful and quiet in the moonlight, then the call of killers riding the wind. Well, Mr. Sam, fetch your cubs. Let's shut them up and get to bed."

The next day was Tuesday. Jed and Randy knocked off work early. The Sunday before, Henry and Jed had agreed that the boys should take Wednesday off and hunt elk. Randy was to sleep Tuesday night at the Martin cabin.

He set off at four that afternoon. Pepper stepped out briskly, tossing his head. Randy drew a deep breath. There was the smell of autumn in the air. Beside a big pine he spied a fat red squirrel busily burying a pine nut against coming blizzards. From high overhead came a faint honking, and he looked up and saw the dark, drawn-out wedge of flying geese.

"Heading for Texas already," he muttered aloud.

Pepper splashed through Grizzly Creek, then broke into a lope out across the pasture. Randy pulled the roan to a walk as they threaded the winding trail through the gap. They splashed through the ford, the current boiling up around the stallion's belly. He scrambled up out of the stream, water running from his sides, and set out at a lope up the long slope to the Martin cabin. Randy could see Hal and Susie waiting out front. He grabbed off his Stetson and waved it over his head.

After an early supper the boys carried buffalo robes out onto the porch and rolled up, pulling the heavy hides snug around their ears against the cold. Long after Hal was asleep, Randy lay awake. The moon came up in the east. From high on the mountains a timber wolf again began its melancholy, howling chant to the moonlight. Randy shivered. For a moment he longed for the hard feel of Pard's body snuggled against his back. Then he caught the comforting sound of Pepper cropping grass close by and relaxed, smiling.

Drowsily he gazed up at the timbered side of Elk Mountain. Moonlight flooded open parks between stands of pine, flooded the foothill slope where the

Martin herd grazed peacefully. The boy's eyelids drooped. He slept.

Up on Elk Mountain where moonlight struggled feebly through needled branches, the dark form of a grizzly moved swiftly and noiselessly through the timber, quartering down the slope toward the grazing Martin herd.

In a burnout the grizzly halted. The massive head came up, swinging slowly from side to side. Black snout wrinkled, testing the air. On the west wind came the warm animal smell of cattle, tantalizing, tempting. The grizzly coughed. His big teeth chopped. Hunger was a gnawing pain in his belly.

Stealthily the giant bear crept out onto a knoll overlooking the pasture slope. He stood up on his hind legs, peering over the bushes at the dark forms of cows drifting slowly over the grass twenty yards below. His black nostrils flared. Slobber dribbled from his gaping jaws.

Suddenly the west wind brought a new smell, a rank stench mingled with the cattle smell. The bear peered nearsightedly at the drifting forms below. Bloodshot eyes fastened on the dark shape of a mountain lion creeping like a shadow through a thicket of chokecherries, belly hugging the ground, glowing amber eyes fixed on a heifer grazing close beyond the thicket.

The lion halted, crouching between two bushes. Its body flattened, head between extended forepaws, haunches bunched, tail tip switching. Suddenly the heifer lifted her head from the grass. For a moment she stared back at the herd slowly grazing downslope, then turned and set out after them at a lumbering trot.

The lion sprang. Two long bounds carried it close to the heifer. The tawny body shot through the air, landed on the heifer's back. Long fangs snapped shut on her neck. The heifer's bellow died away in a gurgle. She stumbled, went down.

The grazing cattle panicked. Bellowing, they stampeded downslope.

The bear's massive head turned for a moment toward the plunging, bellowing cows, then swung back. The heifer had stopped kicking. The lion seized one shoulder in its teeth and dragged the carcass up toward timber. The grizzly dropped to all fours and skulked after the lion, keeping to the shadows of the trees. When the lion stopped beneath a bushy spruce, the bear stopped fifty feet back. His pink tongue licked out at his black nostrils. The grizzly watched as the lion stretched out beside the carcass and began to feed.

The stampeding cattle came sweeping down

around the Martin cabin. Hoofs pounded. The cabin shook. Windows rattled. On the porch, Randy and Hal scrambled out of their buffalo robes. Dazed, they stared out into the moonlight at the dark stream of plunging cows.

Henry Martin stumbled out onto the porch carrying his boots. He yanked his britches up around his middle, his face mottled with anger.

"Reckon what spooked them?" Hal asked him.

His father stomped his feet into his boots. He glared at the seething stream of backs and tossing horns. "Some fool heifer saw her shadow in the moonlight," he growled. "Don't take more'n that."

The main herd was past. Dust hung thick, swirling and lifting in the moonlight. Close beside the cabin Randy glimpsed a dark patch on the ground. Henry had spotted it, too. He jumped down off the porch, the boys at his heels. The dark patch was the trampled carcass of a calf.

"Lord knows how many calves this cost us," Henry said darkly. "Hal, you and Randy check and see if the horses broke their hobbles. Come daylight, we got to cover every foot of the slope. Don't want to leave no dogies or crippled cows."

In the cabin Sarah had the coffee kettle over the fire. Susie came running as her father and the boys entered. "What spooked the cows, Pa?" she cried.

Her father stomped past her. "Don't know," he growled. "All we know is our herd is scattered all over the valley and still running. Coffee ready, Sarah?"

There was no more sleep that night. With the first streak of gray in the east, the boys went out to saddle the horses.

"You saddle Queenie, too," Susie called from the porch. "Pa says I can ride up with you."

They started out at dawn. They rode slowly up through the pine and spruce above the cabin. The morning was gray. The wind blew cold.

On the slope the riders spread out, riding slowly up across the pasture. It was Susie who spotted the crippled steer. Her call brought the others.

Henry Martin sat looking down at the big steer sprawled awkwardly on the ground, its forelegs broken. The steer lifted its head, eyes glaring under oxbow horns.

"A thousand pounds of prime beef," Henry said grimly. He eased his rifle out of the saddle boot and swung down from his horse. The rifle cracked. The steer's head slumped, a hole between the eyes.

Henry ejected the cartridge from his rifle. "You reckon your Pa could spare me the day?" he asked Randy. "There'll be no hunting for you boys today.

I'll need all hands to butcher this steer and round up the herd."

"Sure, Mr. Martin. You want I should ride after him?"

"Later," Henry said heavily, climbing into the saddle. "First, we got to cover the pasture."

They scattered out. Randy sent Pepper up toward the fringe of pines at the top of the slope. There was brush there, chokecherry thickets. Randy held the stallion outside the brush, scanning the ground as he rode along. As he rounded a clump of chokecherry bushes, the stallion hunkered back on his haunches, whinnying.

Randy's eyes swept the ground, lighted on a patch of trampled grass. He forced Pepper toward it, the stallion dancing sideways, eyes rolling.

It was then that Randy spotted the flattened drag marks on the grass, the telltale brown streaks. "Mr. Martin!" he shouted. "Mr. Martin!"

Henry Martin gave an anguished grunt when he saw the brown streaks. He yanked out his rifle and thumbed back the hammer, then spurred his horse up along the drag marks. The youngsters crowded their horses after him.

Beneath the drooping branches of a spruce they rode upon a long mound of freshly dug dirt covered with leaves and moss, dead limbs pulled up over it.

Tracks crisscrossed the loamy earth around the tree.

The riders jumped to the ground and bent over the tracks. Henry Martin shoved his Stetson to the back of his head and spat. "Bear tracks," he said flatly.

"Not just bear tracks," Randy cried. "Spook's tracks! See—" and he pointed to one huge track— "there's the track of his crippled paw."

They dragged the limbs off the cache, kicking away dirt and leaves. "A heifer," Henry Martin grated. "That lousy, cattle-thieving devil got one of my heifers."

Three hours later, Randy rode back with his father. Jed knelt down beside the partly eaten carcass. He lifted the head by its horns, turned it, then let it fall. He ran blunt fingers along the spine at the base of the skull, then looked up at Henry. "See the teeth marks here at the base of the critter's head? They weren't made by no bear. A lion brought the heifer down."

"But what about the grizzly tracks?" Henry demanded.

"Spook stuffed his belly on your beef," Jed told him, "and it's plain to see Spook buried the carcass. Lions don't dig holes and bury under dirt. It's my thinking Spook drove the lion off after the cat made the kill." He got to his feet. "If I'm right, we ought to find lion tracks somewheres about."

Susie found the tracks ten yards up the slope in a patch of soft loam. "Pa!" she called shrilly. "Mr. Reynolds! Here's tracks just like our old tomcat made back home, only lots bigger."

They hurried to her. Randy's eyes widened as he studied the big splayed pad marks. He had seen cougar tracks in the Brasada, but not this big. He glanced up at the trees.

"No use looking," his father told him. "That lion's well away, and the grizzly, too."

"Reckon Spook'll come back to feed again, Pa?"

"Maybe, maybe not. Can't never tell."

"I got two grizzly traps down to the cabin," Henry told him. "Sixteen-inch jaws. Bought them cheap off an old trapper down to St. Louis."

"Bet he was proud to be shet of them," Jed replied. "From what Ben Waters told me, grizzly traps seldom catch grizzlies. Heck of a lot of trouble setting them, and nine times out of ten the grizzly'll outsmart you."

Henry's jaw set stubbornly. "I got a hunch that bear's coming back to finish off the heifer. I'll be much obliged, Jed, if you'll help me set my traps. I don't know the first thing about them."

Jed shrugged. "I'll help. Hope you bought clamps

off your old trapper. We've got to have clamps."

"I got the clamps," Henry assured him, turning to his horse. "Anything else I should fetch up?"

"Your axe, and a rawhide. Soak the rawhide first. And bring a hatchet."

By the time Henry returned dragging two huge rusty steel traps at the end of a lariat, Jed and the youngsters had snaked down half a dozen blown-down logs to the carcass. The men took turns with the axe, felling a dozen limber pines. As fast as the trees toppled, Randy and Hal lopped off the branches with the hatchet.

Jed took charge then. Under his direction they built a V-shaped log pen around the carcass, lashing the logs to three-foot-high stakes with strips of raw-hide, and anchoring the narrow end to the spruce. When the sides were finished, Jed fastened the clamps to the rusty springs of one trap and opened it. With the hatchet he dug a shallow hole in the center of the pen and eased the trap down into it.

"You boys fetch me a good-sized log for a clog," he ordered. When they brought it, he fastened it to the rusty trap chain close beside the carcass.

"Randy, you and Hal lay that pole there across the wide end of the trap," he directed. "That's good. Now we need a couple dozen sticks a foot long and sharp at both ends. Cut them off those limbs there."

"What in tarnation are the sticks for?" Henry asked.

"To drive in the ground both sides of the pole. Won't be no place for Spook to set his feet down, except square on the pan of the trap." He raised his voice. "Boys, cut three or four dozen." He looked at Henry. "We've still got to set the other trap. What about outside the pen, down at the east end? That way, if Spook backtracks, he'll hit it for sure."

When all was to his liking, Jed covered the trap in the pen with dirt and pine needles, then cautiously removed the clamps. "All of you stay outside the pen," he ordered. "A trap like this'll do murder."

He set the second trap outside the pen at the east end. When he had chained it to a log drag, he pulled off his Stetson and wiped his sweaty forehead with his sleeve.

"Well, Henry, there they be. But don't be surprised if Spook don't come back."

"I got my hunch," Henry insisted stubbornly.

Jed grinned. "Sure hope that hunch works all the way, then, so if the grizzly does come back, he won't tear down the pen to get at the bait. Or if you do catch him, we better hope he don't carry off the trap and clog with him. You'd never see hide nor hair of your trap again, and we'd have us a mad, wounded grizzly roaming the mountains."

14 GRIZZLY TRAP

The full moon hung low in the west that night when the grizzly returned to his cache. He slipped stealthily down through the timber, shaggy head swinging from side to side. He was downwind from the carcass. The west wind blew strong up from the valley, bringing the smell of the dead heifer to his nostrils.

151

Where the timber began to thin the grizzly kept to the shadows, stopping often, sniffing uneasily. He emerged from the timber fifty feet above the cache. He halted, his nose wrinkling, then rose on hind legs and peered nearsightedly down at the strange pen.

Cautiously he came down the slope, circling wide around the pen, stopping every few feet, nose testing the air. Opposite the opening he halted. After a moment he approached warily and snuffled over the pole that lay on the ground. He backed away uneasily, turned, shuffled off a few yards.

He stopped, massive head swinging around. His belly churned with hunger. Saliva drooled from his black jaws. He turned back, shambled along the pole across the opening, followed down outside the east wall of the pen.

Close to the spruce he brought up short. His neck stretched out. He snuffled over the ground where the outside trap was buried, then backed off with a muttered growl and circled wide around tree and trap and log drag.

He shambled up along the west side of the pen. Five feet from the spruce he reared up, resting his forepaws on the top log. Sniffing, he peered over at the uncovered carcass. He licked his chops. Bending over the wall he stretched out his right foreleg, straining to reach the carcass. He chopped his teeth, crowding his great hulk against the logs. His long, curved claws touched the carcass, but could not get a grip. He drew back, swung one leg over, and rolled into the pen.

He seized the neck of the carcass in his teeth and lifted it out of the hole. He took one step toward the open end of the pen and stopped. For a moment he stood still, black nostrils spread, beady eyes peering about suspiciously.

Suddenly he swung back, dragging the carcass. Halfway to the spruce he halted. He stood up on his hind legs and lifted the carcass with his teeth to the top of the wall. He shoved it over. It landed with a dull thud. He listened, furry ears pricked forward. Then he vaulted the wall.

Outside he grabbed up the carcass in his teeth and took one step. A loud clank split the stillness of the night. Hot pain seared his right foreleg. His foot was fast in the powerful jaws of the huge steel trap.

He dropped the carcass and lunged forward with a roar. The heavy log drag at the end of the chain flew up and hit his hind legs. He staggered, then flopped snarling to the ground, biting the chain, chewing the log, tearing at the trap with his teeth. When he could not get rid of the tormenting vise biting into his foot he rose and started up toward timber, dragging the trap and the heavy log at the end of the clanking chain.

For two hundred yards he blundered blindly up through the trees. Then the log drag caught in a clump of saplings and stopped him. Spook crashed back through the slender trunks. He tore the saplings out of the ground by their roots. He rose on his hind legs. With his free forepaw he grabbed up the log drag and tucked it under his arm. Then clutching the trap to his chest he started up the mountain, walking like a man carrying a heavy burden.

Soon he stopped to rest on a bed of pine needles. He squatted down on his broad stomach, biting and clawing at the trap and chain.

The moonlight faded. The sky in the east grayed with the dawn. The pulsing pain in his foot drove Spook on. He shuffled awkwardly up through the trees, dragging trap and log.

He squeezed between two big pines. The drag caught. Spook's wild lunges wedged the log firmly against the trunks. His claws dug into the turf. He lunged against the chain, harder, harder, coughing, grunting. The rusty links tautened. Panting, the grizzly rested. After a little he heaved to his feet. He lunged forward. Rusty links strained. Again he lunged. A rusty link snapped. The grizzly crashed to the ground with a furious roar. He was free of the drag.

He struggled to his feet. The trap still held his foot in its vise. He staggered up the mountain, the trap snagging and jarring on stumps and rocks. After a hundred yards, he was forced to rest. He crept in under the branches of a fir that grew beside a boulder and stretched out against the rock, his flanks heaving. The trapped foot throbbed.

After a while he went on. He tired quickly and made a bed in the sand between two boulders. He was panting. Slaver dripped off his tongue. The pain in the trapped foot was a torment. He bit savagely at the trap, but it held.

With a maddened roar he stumbled to his feet. He reared up. He raised his forepaw high and smashed the rusty trap down against a boulder. Again and again he smashed it against the rock, with all the strength of his gigantic hulk. His wild roars reverberated. Blood stained the boulder.

Slowly the trap yielded. One spring broke off, then the other. The jaws opened. The foot tore free.

Spook turned and fled blindly on three legs up through the trees. Beside a narrow stream he bedded down, licking his wound, dabbling the throbbing paw in the icy water. His belly rumbled with hunger. He chopped his teeth viciously. He was trembling

with exhaustion. His head sank wearily on his forepaws, and he slept.

All that day and that night and the following day
Spook nursed his wound. He had nothing to eat but
a few grubs he found under rocks and some half-
ripened chokecherries. By the second night the hunger in his belly was a tormenting fury. At midnight
he rose stiffly and started out through the timber,
walking on three legs. He struck an old game trail
winding below the crest of Elk Mountain and followed along it until he emerged onto the saddle
ridge leading to Moccasin Peak.

He was half a mile from the Reynolds cabin when
he stopped beside a flat rock. Hooking the claws of
his left forepaw under the rim, he heaved it over.
Greedily his tongue licked up the beetles scurrying
underneath. When he had devoured the last, he
limped on.

He stopped on the bank of a tumbling mountain
stream. When he had drunk, he dabbled his throbbing paw in the water. Suddenly his head lifted,
black nose working. The wind had shifted. Now it
came swooping down out of the northwest, scudding
gray clouds before it, hiding the moon.

Thunder cracked. Jagged forks of lightning
slashed the sky. There was a sharp spatter of rain,
the sting of sleet. Spook pushed his way under the

low branches of a spruce and curled up on a bed of needles. He gave a long sighing grunt. His eyes closed.

When he awoke, the storm had ceased. Moonlight glistened on spruce boughs coated with ice. The wind howled in short gusts out of the west, tossing the branches with sharp crackles. Spook sat up on his haunches, pushing his nose into the wind. Hunger was a torment.

Suddenly over the snap and pop of ice-coated branches came the faint bawling of a calf. Spook's ears pricked forward. He lumbered to his feet. Again, the faint bawling. The huge body tensed. Yellowed teeth chopped.

The bawling came again. With a low rumbling growl Spook struck out down the mountain side, a furtive shadow slipping through the timber. He reached the edge of the clearing where Jed and Randy had felled the pines and stopped in a scattering of stumps, nose testing the air. He peered down at the barn and corral at the bottom of the slope. He stood up on his hind legs, his red-rimmed eyes glaring.

The bawling came again. Spook licked his chops. He got down on his belly, slunk in and around through the stumps down toward the bottom of the slope. He reached the corral and stopped. He raised up against the fence, both forepaws on the top, and scrambled over.

A fitful gust swooped down from Moccasin Peak, rolling a wooden bucket with noisy clatter across the corral. The grizzly left off feeding, raised his head. Suddenly a dog barked. Spook's head swung toward the cabin. The dog barked again. The grizzly lowered his head, clamped his teeth on the carcass of the white calf, and lifted it. He carried the carcass to the fence on the north side of the corral and clambered over.

He was halfway up to the stumps in the clearing when the stillness was rent by the shrill tonguing of dogs in the canyon below. The grizzly kept going. He reached the clearing and halted, swinging around. He listened to the frenzied barking of the dogs. In the moonlight he saw them racing toward the corral, saw the running figures of men close on their heels. The grizzly turned and set out up the mountain at a run.

Jed and Randy caught up with the dogs. They were milling along the north fence of the corral. Suddenly they tore out up Moccasin, still tonguing.

"Around to the gate," Jed panted, thumbing back the hammer of his rifle.

They raced around to the gate, swung it open.

"The cow!" Randy choked. "Mrs. Friendly Old Girl!"

The cow lay in front of the barn. The gaping hole in her side showed plainly in the moonlight. Jed and Randy ran across to her. In the mud around the carcass was a maze of bear tracks.

Jed squatted down. "Grizzly," he said flatly.

"I don't see Mr. Sam's calf," Randy panted.

Jed got up. He followed the grizzly's tracks to the fence. He pointed to muddy prints at the base. "Spook," he said bitterly. "Spook did his own cow killing this time. Here's where the devil went out. Toting the calf, you can bet your life."

"We going to follow the dogs?" Randy asked eagerly.

"In the dark?" his father asked harshly. "That grizzly'll lose the dogs the minute he hits timber line. They won't stand a chance of baying him."

"But, Pa—"

"Randy, there ain't no use us losing our heads. Spook's turned cattle killer. Ben Waters said that once a grizzly tastes beef, nothing ain't going to stop him from killing but a bullet. Don't fret, Randy. We'll get Spook in good time. Right now, we've got to break the bad news to Mr. Sam. He's going to take this hard, poor little tyke."

15 MR. SAM IS HURT

Along Grizzly Creek the green of willows and cottonwoods had softened to yellow. Above Bear Claw Canyon the mountain slopes were a riot of green and gold and crimson. The first snow had fallen at timber line. Peaks glistened white in the sunlight. In late afternoon gray clouds scudded across the blue of the sky, clustering around the peaks, darkening, with jagged flashes of lightning, mutterings of thunder.

Since the night the grizzly had struck down cow and calf inside the corral, Jed had driven himself and Randy relentlessly. Day after day they were in the saddle by sunup, headed up Beaver Canyon toward Vanished Longhorn Meadow. They hunted wild cows as men hunt wild animals, roping them, fighting them, tying them. Day after day Pablo and Pancho dragged bawling, struggling wild cows down across the canyon to the gate of Little Brasada corral.

Jed Reynolds rarely smiled now. Two vertical lines were etched deep between his brows. Even the fact that he and Randy had finally caught the wild black bull he coveted gave him only passing pleasure, for again and again the grizzly Spook was raiding the Martin herd or his own.

Spook struck the Martin herd more often, for the leopard dogs prowled Bear Canyon from dusk to dawn. Yet seven times Spook had outwitted the dogs. Seven times Jed and Randy had ridden on carcasses in the canyon, guided to them by the ominous circling of ravens.

"We've got to do something!" Randy burst out that last time, when they stood over the carcass of a mossyhorn cow. "We can't just stand by while Spook kills off our herd."

"We'll get him," his father said grimly. "Between us and the Martins, we'll get him. You heard what Henry said Sunday. Him and Hal are sleeping days and riding herd nights."

"They won't ever get Spook," Randy said positively.

"Now Henry's given up trying to trap him, he just might bring Spook down with a lucky shot."

"I still wish we'd track him with the dogs."

"Catching cows comes first," Jed said shortly. "Our time's running out. Snow'll hit the foothills any day now. When it does, we're through cow catching till spring."

The nights had grown colder in Bear Claw Canyon. Mornings were crisp, but by noon the canyon floor basked drowsily in the warmth of the sun.

Along Grizzly Creek the berry bushes were heavy with fruit. Day after day Molly and Mr. Sam picked pails brimming full, to be made into pies and jam or cooked down with sugar and stored for the winter. At night the cabin was filled with the fragrance of berries bubbling in the pot.

"You got most enough put by for the winter, Molly?" Jed asked one evening, smacking his lips over fresh berry pie.

"Couple days more picking," she told him, "if

the pesky bears leave us that many."

Mr. Sam looked up from his pie, blue eyes twinkling, mouth ringed with purple juice. "My babies are plumb partial to berries," he chuckled. "You ought to see Topsy and Turvy, Pa. They're the cunningest things, sitting up on their back ends and pulling branches down with their paws. They stuff till their bellies pooch out round like punkins. Then they curl up under a bush and snooze."

"At least we don't have to feed them much, long as the berries are ripe," his mother said. "Jed, when do you reckon Sarah will be over to pick?"

"Henry said Sunday she and Susie'd be over this week."

"I aim to take Susie fishing when they come," Mr. Sam announced. "I got my worms dug. Can I tote my gun, Pa?"

"You don't touch that rifle unless me or your Ma or Randy's with you," his father said sharply.

"But what if we happen on that old Spook?"

"Spook don't prowl our canyon by day. You leave Spook to me and Randy. Come along, let's put the cubs to bed."

It was late next afternoon when Jed and Randy rode slowly back from Vanished Longhorn Meadow. They were bone-tired. They had taken Pancho up that morning, had started him home with a mossy-horn cow they had had tied to a tree for two days. Afterwards, they had put in a long afternoon hunting wild cows, but had left only one brindled heifer tied to a tree in the timber.

They rode out onto a knoll overlooking Grizzly Creek and reined up. Their horses slumped tiredly. The dogs flopped down at their feet, tongues lolling.

Randy hooked a knee around his saddle horn, easing sideways in the saddle. He shoved back his Stetson. His eyes swept the valley canyon. Suddenly he straightened up. Far down toward the willows that fringed the creek, dust rose in puffs along the trail. Randy shaded his eyes with his hand. "By golly, Pancho's drug that mossyhorn cow back to the canyon already!" he exclaimed.

"Good neck ox," Jed grunted. He eyed the valley worriedly. "With that cow, I make it we've got ninety head left now. That's counting the brindled heifer we left tied. I've got my heart set on making it an even hundred before snow flies. Twice what we hit Wyoming with."

"And forty cows bred—" Randy reminded him.

"It's a start," his father nodded. "Makes a man want to say his prayers, getting a break like that for his family. Especially if—" he broke off, gazed out over the canyon.

"Specially if Spook don't hit us hard before winter," Randy finished slowly.

"He won't," Jed said harshly. "The day we round up our hundred head, we're going after that grizzly. Going before he gets a chance to den up. Come on, let's ride."

They rode slowly down the trail, the dogs following.

"There's a wagon and team at the cabin," Randy pointed.

"Reckon Sarah and Susie finally made—" Jed broke off, reined up. "What in tarnation's got into Pancho? He's dragging that mossyhorn back up this way."

"No, look, Pa, he's swinging west up the creek. He's going to kill that cow, dragging her fast like that."

"Something's wrong," Jed said shortly. "Come on."

They sent their horses down toward the creek at a gallop, the dogs close on their heels. By now Pancho had dragged the bawling cow fifty yards west up the creek bank. The horses were almost to the willows when Jed and Randy heard the scream of a child—thin, wavering.

"That sounded like Susie," Randy cried.

Jed hit Corker with his spurs. The sorrel lunged

into a run. Randy spurred after him. The horses crashed headlong into the willows.

Jed threw out a warning hand and reined Corker back on his haunches. Randy pulled Pepper to a stop. They looked about frantically. They could hear nothing but the panting of the horses, the rush of the stream. Then from somewhere in the willows came the shrill neighs of horses, the pound of hoofs, and again the thin, frightened scream of the child.

Randy looked at Jed. His father's face was white. He sat bent forward in the saddle, one hand cupping his ear. Randy's eyes swept the willows. Suddenly he gasped and grabbed at his father's arm. "Grizzly!" he stammered. "At the bend in the trail!"

Jed's mouth dropped open. Thirty yards ahead a huge grizzly stood raised on hind legs, watching them. At that moment the dogs caught the scent, broke into shrill yelps. The bear gave one blasting growl, then dropped down and was gone, a dark hulk crashing through the willows. The dogs streaked after him, deep voices yammering back.

Jed and Randy spurred for the creek. They rode out into the churning water. Above the slap of current against boulders, they could hear the voices of the dogs fading away to the east.

Jed led the way west up the bed of the stream. The horses slipped and stumbled on the rocky bottom.

Jed and Randy scanned the banks. Willows swayed gently in the wind.

Jed cupped his mouth with his hand. "Halloo!" he shouted. "Halloo!" He waited. There was no sound but the splash of current against rock. He tried again. "Mr. Sam! Mr. Sam! Susie! Mr. Sam!"

Randy strained to hear. There was only the rush of the creek.

Jed led the way up out of the water into the willows on the far bank. They dismounted, ground-reining the horses. They started walking west along the bank, thrusting their way through the willows, scanning the ground.

"Mr. Sam! Mr. Sam!" Jed called.

Randy shivered. He shouldered a willow aside. He was looking straight through a gap in the thicket. "Pa," he cried, "look, the horses!"

Far up the canyon Poca and Susie's Queenie were galloping toward the cabin, saddles empty.

Jed made a sound deep in his throat. "Come on," he said harshly. "We'll follow that cowpath there. Hurry."

They raced along the winding path. They broke out into a little clearing thick with berry bushes and stopped short, staring. Broken branches hung from bushes. The earth was crisscrossed with the deep ovals of horseshoes, the huge tracks of the grizzly. They crouched over the tracks.

"It was Spook," Jed muttered, pointing to the print of a huge back paw. "I ought to have known that devil's face when I saw it. Come on, we've got to find the young'uns."

They followed the grizzly's tracks along the winding path through the bushes. Suddenly Randy stopped, grabbed his father's arm. "Pa, listen. Somebody's crying."

They started to run. They burst out into a clearing. On the far side stood Susie, knee-deep in berry bushes. She was sobbing in deep wailing gasps.

Jed leaped forward. "Susie," he called. "Susie!"

For a moment the little girl stared uncomprehendingly. Then she gave a cry and stumbled toward them. They met in the middle of the clearing. Jed dropped to his knees. Susie reached out to him with both arms. He hugged her tight. "There, there, honey, you're all right now," he murmured.

Randy, watching, swallowed hard.

"Where's Mr. Sam, Susie?" Jed asked gently. "Don't cry, honey. The bear's gone. Where's Mr. Sam?"

"I don't know," the little girl wailed.

"What happened?" Jed begged. "Where did you lose Mr. Sam?"

"Mama and Mrs. Reynolds went back to the cabin," she gulped. "Me and Mr. Sam stayed here. I was eating berries. Mr. Sam was sitting right over there on Poca. All at once Poca reared up and Mr. Sam was hollering at her and then Queenie started squealing and rearing and broke her tether and Poca bolted with Mr. Sam, and I was here all by myself," she finished with a wail.

"What'd you do then?" Jed demanded.

"I hollered," she hiccoughed. "And then I heard a smacking and a chomping back of me, and I turned around and there was a great big grizzly bear! Sitting right there behind me, raking berries into his mouth and just looking at me!"

"Then what?"

"Then I tried to holler," she gulped, "and the holler wouldn't come, and then I did holler and the bear got up on his hind legs and looked at me. I could see his great big snout moving. And then he got down again and walked off towards the creek."

Gently Jed loosed her arms and stood up. "Take her hand, Randy. We've got to find our boy."

They started out abreast, Jed and Randy holding the child's hands. Susie stumbled along between them, not crying now, breathing in shuddering gasps. They followed the cowpath as it wound around through the bushes. The trail twisted left, then right, and led out into a small clearing.

Susie screamed. Jed and Randy dropped her hands and leaped forward. In the middle of the clearing lay the crumpled body of Mr. Sam.

Jed reached him first. He flung himself down beside the still figure. Mr. Sam's eyes were closed. Blood trickled down his forehead. He was breathing raggedly. One leg was twisted under him.

Randy crouched down beside his little brother. He shivered at the puckered flesh of the knee which showed through a long rent in the faded levis.

"The grizzly's killed him!" Susie wailed.

"He's alive, God be blessed," Jed said softly.

"His leg's broke, ain't it, Pa?" Randy whispered.

Jed nodded. "Wet your kerchief, Randy."

With trembling fingers, Randy fumbled loose the canteen at his belt. He soaked the kerchief. Jed took it and gently sponged away blood and grime from the little boy's face. "Mr. Sam," he said softly. "Mr. Sam."

The little fellow did not open his eyes. His chest rose and fell with his jagged breathing.

Jed turned. "Ride for the cabin, Randy. Tell Ma to gather up all the quilts we've got. Tell her and Sarah to fetch them down in the wagon. Don't you come back, Randy. You ride for Henry Martin!"

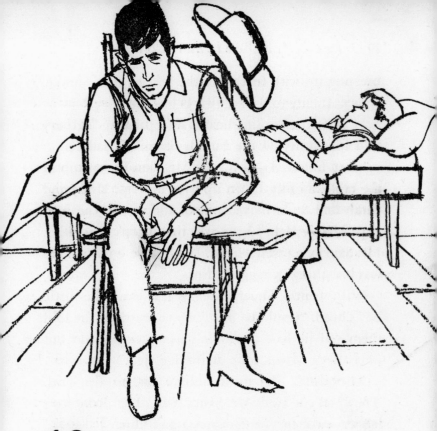

16 END OF THE VIGIL

Dusk was falling when Randy galloped in with
Henry and Hal. The cabin door flung open. Jed
stood in the lamplight.

"Thank God, you've come," he said as they swung
to the ground.

"How is the boy, Jed?" Henry asked.

"Still unconscious. Tossing and screaming and

burning up with fever. It's the left leg that's broke. I guess Randy told you. Just below the knee."

"I've fetched splint boards and padding," Henry told him, untying the bundles from his saddle.

They followed Jed inside. Mr. Sam lay on top of the table, a quilt drawn up over his legs. Molly and Sarah and Susie moved out of the way as the men approached. Henry bent over the unconscious child. Mr. Sam's eyes were closed. His lips were parted. He was breathing in ragged gasps.

With gentle fingers Henry felt over the little boy's head. "Could be he's got a concussion," he told them. "If he has, there ain't much we can do but pray. Let's have a look at the leg, Jed."

They lifted the quilt. Randy bit his lip hard. They had cut away Mr. Sam's levis. The little boy's leg was swollen, the flesh black and blue.

Henry probed the puffy flesh with gentle fingers. "A clean break. You want I should do the setting, Jed? It's one thing I'm good at."

"I'd be obliged." Jed's face was haggard in the lamplight. "I blame myself for this, Henry. I knew all along I ought to leave off cow catching and go after that grizzly. If that bear's killed my little boy—"

"You done what you figured was best," Henry said bluntly. "Boys, lay out the splints and padding handy here on the table. I want you two to hold the lamps close. Now Jed, get a good grip on that leg at the knee, and hold it steady."

Randy stared at the sure movements of Henry's big calloused hands. He gulped when he heard the bone slip into place.

"The padding and splints, Sarah," Henry grunted. "Steady with the lamps, boys. Molly, the bandages."

Deftly he bandaged the splinted leg. It was done. He straightened up. "You can leave go now, Jed."

Jed stepped back. His forehead was beaded with sweat. "We're obliged to you, Henry," he said huskily.

"You just say a prayer the good Lord'll break the fever," Henry said gruffly. "Let's get the tyke in the bunk. Best way to fight his fever is to keep him sponged down with cold water. Molly, we'll need clean soft rags."

Mr. Sam tossed restlessly on the bunk bed. Molly and Jed sat beside him, sponging his feverish body, moistening his parched lips. The little boy moaned in delirium. "Oh, my leg . . . Spook . . . go away . . . go away . . . oh . . . oh . . . I hurt . . ."

Randy crouched on the floor at the foot of the bunk. The look on his father's face awed him. Jed sat hunched forward. His eyes glittered. His big fists clenched and unclenched. When Henry offered to take his place beside Mr. Sam, Jed shook his head.

"Later, Henry. I'll have need of you later, when I start out after that grizzly. I was just sitting here thinking, Henry. When we set that trap for Spook, we didn't know how soon our fight was coming, did we? Our fight to see who's going to survive in our valley."

At midnight Hal and Susie stretched out on a buffalo robe in front of the fire. Sarah and Henry lay down in the bunk across the cabin.

Randy picked up the water bucket and his gun and went down to the creek. He brought back the brimming bucket and set it down beside his mother. "Mr. Sam's going to get well, isn't he?" he whispered.

His mother looked at him bleakly. "We don't know, Son. The fever's burning him up."

Tears stung the boy's eyes. He knelt down beside the bunk, locking his hands together, pressing them hard against his trembling mouth.

Suddenly Mr. Sam screamed. "Spook . . . go away . . . I'll shoot you . . ."

Jed groaned. He slid to his knees beside Randy. Molly knelt down beside them. They bowed their heads. For a moment there was silence, broken only by the whimpering of the unconscious child. "I hurt . . . Ma . . . I hurt . . . I want my Ma . . ."

"Kind Father in Heaven," Jed prayed softly, "have

mercy on us in our hour of need. Spare us our little boy. He—" His voice broke in a strangled sob.

The night dragged on. Hour after hour Mr. Sam tossed and moaned. "Oh . . . my head . . . Spook . . . my head . . ."

When the sky showed gray at the windows, Randy picked up the water bucket and stumbled out onto the porch. The dogs had come home. They were stretched out limp against the wall.

Nugget and Polky thumped their tails feebly. Pard dragged up, whining. Randy knelt and examined the dogs' paws. "Nothing but what bear grease'll fix up," he told them. He put both arms around Pard's neck and laid his cheek against the rough head. "Tearing out after that grizzly like you could whip him," he choked.

When he carried fresh water into the cabin, Sarah and Henry were up. Henry stood bent over Jed. "We'll watch over him like he was our own," he was saying. "You two have got to get some sleep."

Jed rose stiffly. He rubbed his hand over bloodshot eyes. "Guess you're right," he said dully. "I'll need my wits when I start after that grizzly. Come, Molly. Randy, you best stretch out there beside the young-'uns."

"After a bit, Pa. Poor old Pancho's bawling his

head off down at the Little Brasada. He's held that mossyhorn cow all night outside the gate. I'm going to wake Hal and we'll go down and get the mossyhorn inside the corral."

"I'd forgot the cow," Jed said heavily. "Doesn't seem possible it was only yesterday evening we were watching Pancho haul that wild cow down toward the creek. Seems like a long time ago."

Molly and Jed slept for a couple of hours. Jed awoke first. "How is he?" he asked, sitting up and swinging his legs to the floor.

"Just the same," Sarah murmured.

Henry got up from his chair. "Now you've woke up, Jed, me and Hal will ride along home. Ain't nothing I can do here, and I can't rest easy with that grizzly roaming the valley. We'll be back, come morning."

When they had gone, Molly and Jed took up their vigil beside Mr. Sam. Randy stretched out on the buffalo robe. He tried to shut his ears to the moans of his little brother. "Please, God," he whispered thickly, "please, God." His eyelids drooped. He slept.

It was a cry from his mother that awakened him three hours later. Randy sat up, shaking his head groggily. His parents were bent over Mr. Sam. "He's sweating!" his mother cried. "He's sweating!"

Randy scrambled to his feet. Sarah and Susie were hurrying toward the bunk. Sarah felt Mr. Sam's head. "The fever's broke!" she exclaimed. "Thank God!"

They stood silent while Jed dipped a cloth in cold water and squeezed a few drops into the child's parched mouth. Mr. Sam's throat quivered convulsively as he swallowed. His eyelids fluttered, slowly lifted. The little boy looked up dazedly at the faces bent over him. "My head hurts," he whimpered.

"It'll be better by 'n by," his mother soothed.

Mr. Sam tried to raise up from the pillow. "My leg feels funny," he said weakly. "I can't move it."

"It'll be all right, Mr. Sam," Randy comforted. "You'll be up playing with your cubs in no time."

"I fed the cubs for you," Susie broke in eagerly.

Mr. Sam looked at them. "Where's that old Spook?" he demanded feverishly. "Lemme up from here. Where's my gun?"

"Easy, fellow, easy," Jed murmured, holding the child quiet on the pillow. "Me and Randy'll take care of that bear. That old grizzly ain't going to bother you no more."

Mr. Sam relaxed against the pillow. "I'm hungry," he whimpered.

His mother hurried for a cup of milk. He drank a few sips, then fell fast asleep.

"It's a natural sleep," Sarah reassured them. "He's going to make it now."

Toward noon that day, thunderheads began to boil up over Elk Mountain. The wind blew sharp and cold out of the northwest. Jed eyed the weather worriedly.

"Snow's likely as not to hit by nightfall," he told Randy. "Much as I hate to leave Mr. Sam, I reckon we'd best take Pancho up and get him started down with that brindled heifer."

They set out after dinner. They were back at sundown. Molly came to the door when they rode up to the cabin.

"How is he?" Jed asked anxiously.

"Asleep, thank goodness. He woke up once. I gave him some warm milk, and he dropped right off."

Jed and Randy unsaddled the horses. They carried the saddles up onto the porch. They stood for a moment on the step, shoulders hunched against the cold.

"Best carry the saddles inside,'" Jed decided, eyeing the heavy gray clouds that shrouded the chain of peaks.

"Anyway, you won't have to get out tomorrow if

the weather does turn bad," Molly said hopefully from the doorway.

"Me and Randy are starting out after Spook at sunup," Jed said without looking at her. "Pancho'll have the brindled heifer down by then. Just as soon as we get her into the corral, we're hitting the trail."

Molly did not reply. Randy stole a quick look at her. His mother's face was serene, but there was fear in her eyes. "I'll see about getting food ready for you to take," she said after a moment.

Jed gave her a quick smile. "Good girl."

They turned in right after supper. Jed and Randy rolled up in buffalo robes before the fireplace. Randy fell asleep at once. He was awakened by his mother shaking his shoulder. "Randy! Wake up! Randy!"

He sat up, blinking in the lamplight. His father was yanking on his boots. "Mr. Sam?" Randy stammered.

"Mr. Sam's all right," his father said shortly. "Can't you hear that infernal bawling outside?"

"It's Pancho!" Randy reached for his boots.

"Pancho," his father nodded grimly. "Something's gone wrong. Put on your jacket, Randy. It'll be cold. That lantern ready, Molly?"

She handed him the lantern.

"Fetch your gun, just in case," Jed told Randy.

They stepped out onto the porch. Cold wind hit

them. From the darkness came Pancho's plaintive bawling. Jed lifted the lantern high, gave a snort of disgust. "He's lost the brindled heifer. First time a cow ever broke loose from Pancho."

They went down the steps to the ox. Pancho stood spraddle-legged, head low. The dogs milled around him, whining. It was Randy who said, "Pancho's hurt, Pa."

Jed lowered the lantern until its light shone full on the drooping head. Pancho's nose was torn and bloody. The upswept right horn was streaked with dried blood.

"He's been fighting!" Randy exclaimed.

Jed picked up the frayed rope end dangling from Pancho's neck. He held the lantern close. Randy gave a startled cry. "Look at the gray hairs stuck to his horn, Pa!"

Deliberately Jed plucked one coarse gray hair off the horn and held it close to the light.

"What do you figure, Pa?" Randy asked eagerly.

"I figure Spook got the brindled heifer," Jed said harshly. "From the looks of Pancho's horn, Spook made a swipe at the ox and Pancho gored him."

"Bad, you reckon?"

"No telling. But Randy, this may be our break. Spook will be slowed down. Now we have a real chance to get him."

When they went back into the cabin, Molly took one look at Jed's face. "Spook again," she said quietly.

Jed nodded. "Looks like he got the heifer necked to Pancho. Pancho gored the grizzly. Me and Randy are getting ready. You be all right alone here with Sarah?"

"We'll be all right."

"Henry and Hal'll be back," Sarah reminded. "Oughten you to wait so's they can go along to help?"

Jed shook his head. "Better just me'n Randy. We're used to tracking together. You women rustle up the grub. Enough for a couple of days, anyway."

They all worked. Randy rolled the coffeepot and skillet in the buffalo robes and tied them. He lashed their slickers to the rolls. Then he and his father checked their guns and counted out cartridges. While Sarah and Molly stowed venison and bread in saddlebags, Susie ground coffee and filled a small sack. Molly took down their precious horde of sulphur matches and counted out a dozen. "I'll put these with your flint and steel," she told Jed.

With the first graying of the sky, Randy went out to saddle the horses. Wind knifed down cold out of the north. Storm clouds hung low over Eagle Mountain.

His father brought out the bedrolls. "Storming

up on Eagle," he muttered. He gave one bedroll to Randy, then lashed the other behind Corker's saddle.

"Sure some lightning up there, Pa."

Molly and Sarah came out with the saddlebags and guns. "Mind you two take care," Molly said worriedly.

"We will, girl."

Randy, busy tying his bedroll to his saddle, glanced down toward Grizzly Creek. "Pa," he said urgently, "look at the ravens circling down there by the creek."

Jed swung around. "Blasted scavengers! That'll be where we'll find the carcass of the brindled heifer." He gave Molly a quick kiss and swung into the saddle. "Let's go."

Randy hung back for a moment, hugged his mother hard. Then he hurried to Pepper.

They rode down to the Little Brasada, the dogs trotting silently behind the horses. At the canyon corral, they swung south along the trail made by the neck oxen. Randy rode watching the ravens circling low over the willows. He shivered as he caught their dismal cawing.

They followed the trail into the willows. Suddenly there was a wild beating of wings in front of them, a loud croaking. A dozen ravens rose from behind a clump of willows at a bend in the trail just ahead.

Pard gave one sharp bark and led Nugget and Polky at a run down around the bend. Jed and Randy sent their horses after them.

They rode upon the carcass of the brindled heifer at the edge of the trail. Willows were broken and trampled around it. The dogs were snuffling over the ground with low growls.

Jed and Randy jumped to the ground.

"Stay with the horses," Jed ordered.

Randy watched as his father slowly circled the heifer, then followed along the trail for twenty feet toward the creek. He stopped there for a moment, then came back.

"Ain't hard to see what happened," he told Randy. "Here's the heifer's tracks, hers and Pancho's. See, all at once the heifer crowds Pancho off here into the willows. She was lunging—see how deep her hoofs sink in here? And here's Spook's tracks, coming straight across the trail from the far side. Look over there by that willow clump across the trail. A laying-up bed. Easy to figure what happened. Spook'd come back to the berries. He was laying up there under those willows sleeping, with his belly stuffed. When Pancho brought the brindled heifer along he woke up sudden, got scared. You can see by the carcass it wasn't no hungry bear made that kill. Spook broke the heifer's spine. That's when old Pancho put up his fight to get loose from her. See how the ground's cut up? Hoof and bear tracks on top of each other."

"There go Spook's tracks back across the trail," Randy pointed. "He's heading east for Eagle Mountain."

"And he was bleeding," Jed said with satisfaction. "See the drops on those willow leaves by his tracks?"

Jed turned. "Nugget!" he called. "Pard, Polky!"

The dogs came running, tails beating. Jed stuck their noses in the grizzly tracks. Snuffling noisily, they crossed the trail and followed the tracks into the willows beyond.

17 THE CAVE

Jed and Randy sprinted for their horses and rode
after the dogs. The grizzly had gone plunging into
the willow clumps that bordered the trail. Fifty
yards east of the carcass, Jed and Randy caught up
with the dogs. They were milling along the creek
bank. Jed swung to the ground and pushed them
aside.

"Spook's bleeding bad," he called to Randy. "Looks like he took to the water to soak his wound. Ride on down the bank. See if you can pick up his tracks coming out."

A hundred feet east, the creek made a sharp bend to the left. As Randy rounded the bend, he spotted the grizzly's huge tracks at the water's edge. His shout brought Jed and the dogs. The dogs snuffled noisily over the tracks. Suddenly Pard lifted his head and bayed, then the other two opened. They tore away in full cry, running east toward Eagle Mountain.

Jed and Randy sent the horses at a gallop after them. The rise and fall of the dogs' voices rolled back. They had not covered a mile when the deep-throated baying shrilled.

"They've faulted," Jed growled.

When Jed and Randy rode up, the dogs were milling up and down the bank, whining dismally. Randy rode down along the creek for a hundred yards without picking up the grizzly's tracks. He turned back.

"Spook's crossed over then," Jed grunted. He whistled to the dogs. "We'll pick up his trail on the south bank."

The horses slipped and splashed through the churning water, the dogs lunging ahead. They scrambled out up the rocky bank. It was Pard that nosed out the tracks leading to a laying-up bed back under a clump of willows.

Jed and Randy dismounted. "The cold water didn't stop his bleeding," the boy told his father, pointing to telltale brown smears on the willow leaves lining the bed.

The dogs were away in full cry, quartering southeast across the canyon toward the ridge between Lobo and Eagle. Jed shoved back his hat and scowled up at the sky. A heavy gray overcast blanketed the canyon. Up at timber line on Eagle, thunderheads boiled. Jagged fingers of lightning struck at the barren granite peak. There was an angry rumble of thunder from the cliffs. Then a wall of rain shut the cliffs from their sight.

"If that confounded storm would only let up," Jed muttered. "But storm or no storm, we're not turning back."

"I was dead sure Spook'd head straight up the creek to the waterfall," Randy said puzzledly.

"He's wounded. Likely taking an easier way up. Come on."

They sent their horses at a gallop across the canyon after the dogs. At the foot of Eagle, Spook's trail swung east up into timber. Jed and Randy urged the horses into a hacking gallop up the first grade. In the timber they rode onto an old bear trail angling up around the side of the mountain. The dogs were out of sight up the trail, excited voices yammering back.

For over an hour Jed and Randy followed the trail as it wound through thick stands of pine, out across parks, back into timber again. There was the loud mutter of thunder, the chilling blast of wind, the drum of raindrops on trees. Jed and Randy untied their slickers and struggled into them. They pushed on.

The horses were lathered. They wheezed as they climbed. All at once Jed threw out a warning hand and reined up.

"Trail forks," he called back. "Listen, can you tell which way the dogs are running?"

The deep singing bays of the dogs rolled back down.

"They took to the right," Randy cried.

Jed led the way up the right fork. Suddenly above the rumble of thunder they caught the shrill quickened baying of the dogs.

"They've jumped the bear," Jed said grimly, hitting Corker with his spurs.

Randy sent Pepper flying up the trail after his father. A jagged fork of lightning split the sky. Thunder roared. Flash after flash lit up the trees. Randy scrouged low in the saddle. Rain lashed his face.

They spurred up along the steep trail winding among the pines. Suddenly they burst out of timber into a sodden meadow dotted with clumps of blue spruce. They reined to a sliding, muddy stop.

On the far side of the narrow clearing was a scattering of tall pines. From behind the pines rose a jumble of stacked-up boulders leading up to a rock wall broken by cliffs and rock tables and slides. Stunted spruce and fir grew up out of clefts in the rock.

Over the steady drumming of rain came the frantic barking of the dogs.

"Sounds like they're above us," Jed said, scanning the towering wall across the clearing. He cupped his ear with his hand. "That danged loud roaring—"

"It's the waterfall," Randy said excitedly, then: "Pa, the dogs! Up on the rocks, just left of the top of that dead pine. There's the grizzly—there's Spook! Crossing that rock table up over the dogs! There he goes back of the scrub spruce—there he is—up on the rocks. He's getting away!"

Jed's eyes had found dogs and grizzly. He stared grimly, heedless of the water that poured off the brim of his Stetson.

"The dogs can't even get back down off the rocks," Randy groaned. "And they almost had him! He's got away!"

"That cattle-killing son of Satan led the dogs up there on purpose," Jed said flatly, "knowing he'd lose them. But he didn't figure on me and you."

Randy stared at his father. "What do you mean?"

"We're going up."

"But what if we can't get the dogs up?"

Jed pointed toward the top of the rock wall. "Up there a mite east of where Spook's climbing—see that overhang of rock? See that dark hole under it? I figure that's the mouth of a cave. Just the kind of den a wounded bear'd hole up in. That's where Spook's heading. We're going after him."

Randy rode after his father across the meadow. They tethered their horses to pines. Jed took off his slicker. Randy struggled out of his, shivering in the cold rain. With stiff hands the boy worked his rifle out of the saddle boot. Without a word they strapped their guns across their backs. Only then did the man turn and look directly at the boy.

"We're taking our lives in our hands when we go up those rocks, Son, but we can't stop now. It's us or the grizzly. Watch every step you take. I won't be able to help you if you slip. Come on."

They started over a steep rockslide. Slipping, sliding, crawling, they reached the base of the stacked-up boulders. Above them the dogs whined dolefully.

Jed wedged one boot in a crevice between two

boulders and reached for an outjutting knob of stone. With a swing he reached the rock where the dogs were trapped. He stretched an arm down to Randy and hoisted him up.

The dogs were all over them. Jed roughed their heads, studying the steep climb ahead. Pard reared up against Randy, licking his face, whimpering. The boy gave him a quick hug.

"We'll be back," he whispered.

On their hands and knees Jed and Randy clawed their way up over the boulders. They reached the table rock. Beyond, ledges jutted out from the side of the mountain. Jed pointed to rain-washed blood spots on the first ledge. "Spook's strained open his wound," he told the boy.

They pulled up by runty bushes and outcropping rocks, going on hands and knees. They reached a narrow ledge and rested, panting. Randy risked one quick look down. Far below he could see the black spots that were the dogs. "Must be nigh halfway up to the cave," he panted.

Jed grunted. He raised one hand and pointed toward the top of the wall to the east. Randy glimpsed a dark spot moving up the face of the mountain—the grizzly's back.

There was the mutter of thunder rolling down from the crags. Wind blew in spiteful gusts. Jed and

Randy clawed up over outcropping rock slabs. They crawled out at last onto a wide ledge and stood up, holding to outjutting rocks, scanning the wall for a way up. Against the eerie black sky the rocks stood out ghostly white. Electricity crackled along the edges of cyclone-black storm clouds.

Suddenly a bolt of lightning split the sky open. One blinding prong shot straight down. It hit the craggy rocks above them and kept on bouncing, striking with fire from crag to crag, then blasted the trunk of a tall spruce and the huge boulder at its base. The next second a terrific clap of thunder jarred the wall. The ledge shook beneath them. There came an ominous cracking, a tremendous, prolonged shattering.

"Rockslide!" Jed cried. "Under that shelf there!"

He pushed Randy to the ground and dropped down beside him. They wormed their way on their bellies under the overhang of rock backing the ledge. With deafening roar, broken chunks of granite boulders came cascading down over the ledge. Showers of grit rolled back under the shelf. Then from below came the rumble of falling rocks.

Jed and Randy crawled out from under the shelf and sat up. Jed wiped his gritty face with his sleeve. He looked at Randy and silently shook his head.

They crawled on hands and knees up the wide

swathe cut by the slide. They pulled up by tangled roots of trees toppled by the boulders. They neared the spruce that lightning had struck. The trunk still smouldered.

The mountain side was bathed in greenish light. Icy wind blasted down from the crags. Jed looked at the sky.

"Make for that boulder yonder," he told Randy. "Hail's coming, for sure."

They scrambled on all fours for the lee of the outjutting boulder. Hail stung their backs. They scrouged down under the overhang of rock, faces against knees. The clouds opened. Wave after wave of hail hit the mountain. Crouched miserably under the narrow overhang, Jed and Randy weathered the storm.

Suddenly it was over. They crawled out from their shelter. The mountain side was white with hailstones. They crawled up past the lightning-struck spruce. They clambered up over layers of flat, anchored rocks slick as glass. They scrambled out on top of the wide table rock. Limber pines and firs grew in crowded clumps. Through the trees they saw the black mouth of the cave yawning under an overhanging cliff not twenty feet before them.

They stretched out on the ground, gulping in air, legs quivering.

"There it is," Jed panted, "there's the cave." He looked at Randy. "Going into that cave after Spook is crazy," he said quietly, "and I know it. But I'm fed up. That grizzly's been a plague and a torment to us ever since we moved into Bear Claw Canyon. We just can't pass up our chance to finish him off."

18 END OF THE TRAIL

The wind had died. The rain had stopped. Jed found
a half-rotted blowdown under the pines, dug out
punky wood with his knife, and got a fire going.
They huddled shivering over the blaze, their wet
clothes steaming.

"I've been turning this over in my mind," Jed
said slowly. "We don't know what this cave is like

or where we'll meet up with Spook inside. We've got to have light. That mean's a torch. It'll be safest for you to carry it, Randy. That way, I can cover you from behind."

They decided on a pitchy fir for the torch, a blow-down six feet long. Jed lopped off the branches with his bowie knife. "You'll be carrying the torch ahead of me," he told Randy. "Happens you come on Spook sudden-like, around a corner, say, you shove that torch square in his face. Aim for his nose and eyes. That'll give me a chance to shoot."

"Yes, sir," said Randy nodding; then: "Pa, you hear that cawing?" He looked up at the sky. "A raven," he said pointing, "back up there in the east. Heading this way."

The lone raven circled wide above them, lower and lower. They listened to his hoarse cawing. He dropped closer, lighted on the dead top of a tall pine.

"Danged vulture," Jed growled. He stood up, held the shredded tip of the fir in the flame until it caught. "Douse the fire, Randy."

He walked over to the mouth of the cave and thrust the torch inside. "Tunnel's just barely high enough for us to stand up," he said as Randy came up. "Looks like lots of seepage from the ceiling. That means a slick floor. Take the torch. Hold it high as you can, and move it from side to side, so's we can see the whole tunnel."

Randy took the torch. He waited while Jed checked his rifle, thumbed back the hammer. Then they crept into the tunnel. The silence was broken by the steady drumming of waterdrops from the ceiling. The fetid stink of bear was heavy on the air.

They followed the winding passage for some twenty feet. They reached a sharp bend, stopped, and listened. From the darkness overhead came faint squeaks, the eerie rustling of wings.

"Bats," Jed whispered. "They—" He did not finish. From around the bend came a loud splashing of water. Jed and Randy froze. The splashing came again.

"Come on," Jed hissed. "Watch sharp!"

Side by side they crept around the bend. Randy thrust the torch high. They had emerged into a large cavern with walls rising thirty or forty feet.

Randy caught his breath. In the center of the cavern was a shallow pool. Even as he looked an immense black hulk heaved up out of the water, half raised up on massive hind legs.

"Get the light on him," Jed hissed, snapping his rifle to his shoulder.

At that instant the grizzly dropped with a splash to all fours, plunged out of the pool away from them, and vanished into darkness beyond.

"Lower the torch," Jed barked. "Quick!"

They hurried to the pool. On the rock beside it, drops of blood showed where Spook had gone into the water.

"He went out through that tunnel beyond the pool," Jed grunted.

They circled quickly around the pool, picked up the grizzly's huge wet tracks on the floor, and followed them out into a tunnel with walls eight feet high.

"Keep the torch high, and go slow,'" Jed whispered. "I'll be right behind you."

Step by step Randy moved forward along the winding passage. He stopped at an arch leading into a chamber on the left and shoved the torch through the opening.

"Keep going," Jed hissed as he caught up. "Spook went on. See those water spatters up there ahead on the floor? He's bound to be close by. That stinking bear smell's powerful strong. Remember, Son, if we run on him, shove that torch in his snout."

Randy crept forward along the tunnel. Blood pounded in his ears. His hands trembled. Torchlight danced weirdly on the walls. Around a slight curve was a branching of the tunnel. Just this side, an opening yawned black on the right.

Randy eased up and shoved the torch through, hands shaking.

"Easy there," his father whispered at his shoulder. He reached out with his left hand, and steadied the torch.

They stood there side by side. Randy peered into the chamber. "Looks like it curves back to the right," he whispered.

Suddenly there came a soft scraping sound. Loose pebbles rolled down to their feet. Randy swung the torch to the right. The flame flared; there was the acrid stench of burning hair. An earsplitting roar blasted out of the shadows from beyond the flame. With huge forepaws raised high, wicked claws gleaming in flickering light, the enormous dark hulk of the grizzly towered over the torch.

With a savage roar the beast lunged forward, smashed the torch aside, and crashed between the man and the boy, slamming them against rock walls. Randy felt the hot blast of putrid breath on his face, felt searing pain as claws dug into his shoulder and raked down his left side. Then the grizzly was gone, his vicious growls reverberating from the walls of the tunnel.

Randy opened his eyes. He was lying on his back. Raising one hand, he brushed at the drops of water dripping from the ceiling onto his face. He swallowed convulsively. His left shoulder throbbed agonizingly. His jacket was soggy with blood.

Groggily he pushed himself upright, choking, coughing. Smoke filled the tunnel. The torch lay smoking and sputtering on the ground beside him.

From the darkness came a raspy coughing. "Pa," Randy cried. "Pa, you all right?" He picked up the torch and propped it against the mouth of the tunnel. The flame flared up.

Jed lay sprawled in the opening to the tunnel. Randy crawled to him. His father's face was bloody.

"Wind knocked out of me," Jed coughed, pushing himself up. "Blasted bear stepped square on my face. Wipe the blood away. I can't see."

Randy worked his canteen loose from his belt. He wet his kerchief and sponged away the blood. "It's just a scalp wound, Pa," he panted. "It ain't bad."

Jed reached out. "Your arm!"

"Spook's claws caught my side," the boy said. "Ain't deep."

Jed bound the wet kerchief around his forehead. "Which way did the devil run?"

Randy crawled to the opening into the tunnel. "To the right," he reported. "You can see his tracks in the dust."

Jed shivered. "I could swear I feel wind blowing

on my back." He twisted around. "Look how the torch's flaring. There's air from outside coming in somewhere. See what's up that tunnel across over there."

Randy crawled across to the mouth of the tunnel opposite the opening where they sat. The floor of the tunnel climbed steeply. From high up ahead came a feeble glimmer of daylight.

"It climbs nigh straight up," he called. "I can see daylight at the end. And some sort of a tree."

Jed crawled over to him and peered up. "It's an air hole," he panted. "We're getting out!"

"And not run Spook down?" Randy cried.

"Clawed up like we are, we wouldn't stand a chance," Jed said. "We'll get him, but not in here. Let me have a look at that arm, Randy."

"It's all right," the boy protested, but he knelt quietly while his father examined his wounds.

"Deep scratches," Jed grunted. "The bleeding's about stopped. The Lord was sure with us this time, Randy."

He turned, picked up his rifle, strapped it to his back. "Hand me the torch. You favor that arm all you can."

Jed led the way into the tunnel opposite, crawling on hands and knees, pushing the torch ahead of him. At the base of a steep incline he stopped and tilted his head back. He was looking up toward a wide round hole. Beyond was gray sky.

"We're going to come out through a sinkhole," he panted. "Think you can make it?"

"Sure," Randy wheezed.

Jed doused the torch. He started up, pulling himself along by outjutting rocks. Randy followed close on his heels.

On the rim of the sinkhole towered a dead spruce. The bank had cut away from its roots. They dangled, bare and twisted, down into the tunnel. Jed grabbed a thick root with his left hand, braced his right against a boulder, and shoved up. He felt the boulder move, heard the rattle of rolling rocks.

"Grab the tree roots," he hollered as he heaved himself up over the rim. "The boulder's coming down."

Randy grabbed for the twisted roots and clung. He felt the tree sway, heard the cracking of dead wood. The boulder careened past in an avalanche of loose rock.

Jed reached down and pulled Randy up over the rim. They sprawled out on their bellies in the gravel at the edge of the sinkhole, gulping in air. After a bit Jed eased over and gazed up at the gray sky. "You all right?"

"I'm all right," Randy sat up. "Listen. Hear that

roar? We're back close to the waterfall."

He struggled to his feet and peered about. Over low upjutting boulders twenty feet ahead, he saw the tips of pines tossing in the wind.

"I'm going to see," he panted. He clambered up over the rocks. He reached a wide rocky ledge and sank down, bracing his throbbing shoulder against a rock. "Spook's brought us back to the waterfall, Pa," he called.

Jed pushed himself up. He climbed up over the rocks. He sank down beside the boy.

Below them a hundred yards to the east the seething torrent of muddy water plunged with a savage roar over the fall. Huge logs came hurtling down, shot out over the brink, twisting and turning, and dropped from sight in white water.

"Where are the slabs you crossed over on?" Jed asked.

"Where those two big logs are snagged above the fall. The creek's swollen so big the rocks are under water."

"Must have been a heavy storm higher up. Look at that big spruce windfall coming down the creek."

They watched as the current swung the windfall against the submerged slabs. The huge tree hung there, its upended roots held high out of the water.

"Pa, look, there's that raven again. Flying over the

pines next to the crossing. See how he's circling? Reckon there's a carcass down there?"

His father raised up. "There's something moving down there in the trees. Wait a second till it gets against those rocks— It's a grizzly! It's Spook! That blasted monster got out of the cave before we did!"

"He sure got down there fast!"

"The tunnel he took must have come out on the east," Jed grunted. He yanked his shoulder strap around, unbuckled his rifle. He levered a cartridge into the chamber. "Spook's luck's run out. He ain't getting away this time."

"Pa, look, he's going to try to cross the creek!"

"Then he'll have to climb out on that windfall," Jed said grimly. "That's when I'll drop him."

The grizzly went shambling through the pines, heading toward the crossing. At the edge of the water he reared up on hind legs, lunged forward. He heaved his great hulk up onto the tree, clambering through the twisted roots.

Jed dropped to one knee. Slowly he raised his rifle. Spook broke through the tangle of roots and stepped out onto the trunk. The blast of Jed's rifle split the air. The grizzly tottered. The massive head swung around. He bit at his shoulder.

"Creased him," Jed snapped, levering another cartridge into the chamber and sighting.

"Pa!" Randy cried. "That big log coming down! It's going to ram the spruce!"

A huge log came hurtling down the current, crashed into the spruce where Spook clung, jarred it loose from the rocks, and hurled the grizzly into the foaming water.

The bear's dark head broke surface. He was struggling. He went under, came up again. The next moment the torrent smashed the spruce down upon him. Bear and tree spun crazily, slammed against a jutting rock, and hung there pitching and bobbing, before spinning out again into the current. Then they swept out over the brink, twisting, turning end over end, plunging down in thundering white water.

"The whirlpool under the waterfall," Randy muttered. "Spook'll land in the whirlpool. It's a hundred feet down. He ain't got a chance."

"Thank God," Jed said simply.

"Can we climb down to the whirlpool and find him, Pa?" the boy asked eagerly.

"With us mauled up like we be?" Jed asked shortly. "We'll be lucky to get back down to the dogs and horses and pitch camp before sundown."

"Then what about us climbing up on that table top over there to the east?" Randy asked. "Ain't more'n a hundred feet to the top. We could see the whirlpool from that high up."

"Reckon we could do that much," Jed nodded.

A series of rocky ledges led up to the table top. As they climbed, the thunder of the waterfall grew louder and louder. They reached the top and sank down. Panting, they looked down into the gorge. Fifty yards below to the right the churning water of the creek rushed down, tossing windfallen trees like driftwood over the brink of the fall. The windfalls plummeted down the white cataract and landed in a boiling, seething caldron of water. They were sucked under the center of a tightly spinning whirlpool, were spewed out ten yards below on the boulder-strewn shore.

"Pa," Randy pointed. "There's Spook!"

Against the piled-up logs on the shore lay the up-rooted spruce to which the grizzly had clung. The grizzly lay sprawled on his back against the spruce. Waves swirled up around his motionless body.

"It was him or us," Jed said almost regretfully. "And to think he almost got away. . . . Come on, Son, we've got a long way back."

They turned away. Slowly they clambered over the rocks.

All at once Randy stopped. "Pa, look," he pointed, "through the trees there. Moccasin Peak."

"Sure gives you a good feeling to know Ma and Mr. Sam are there waiting," his father said quietly.

"They'll be proud when we tell them what happened today."

"Not Mr. Sam," Randy grinned. "Mr. Sam's going to be hopping mad. He was plumb set on killing Spook himself. I'll bet the Martins'll still be at the cabin when we get home, Pa. Won't we have us a good time!"

Back down in timber, they stumbled onto an old game trail.

"Looks like this is heading our way," Jed told the boy. "We'll take it."

They followed the trail down through heavy timber. They came out at last on the edge of a small clearing. On the opposite side two tall spruce flanked the trail like giant sentinels. Between the spruce they could see Mocassin Peak.

"Wish we were heading down Moccasin toward the cabin right now," Randy sighed, easing his throbbing shoulder.

At that instant the sun broke through the clouds. Sunlight glistened on Moccasin's snow-capped peak.

"Randy, look!" Jed cried.

High over the distant mountain a rainbow shimmered in the sky. They gazed breathless. The rainbow's arching hues dipped earthward over the mountains.

Randy turned, face glowing. "It's sure some—" he began, then broke off. "Pa, look! There under that spruce. Elk antlers."

"A six-pointer," Jed nodded.

"And still on the skull. Can I take them home, Pa? Mr. Sam'd be proud if I fetched them to him, and I sure would like to have the ivory tusks."

"Don't see why not," Jed said slowly, "if you figure you can tote them down to the horses with that bunged-up arm."

"Sure I can, Pa."

Jed walked over and sat down on a low boulder in the center of the clearing. "Jumping Jehosha-phat," he said tiredly, "but this has been a day. And we ain't through with Spook yet. Tomorrow we've got to find a way down to the carcass. I aim to have that pelt. And I've got it in my mind to give the claws to Mr. Sam. You won't mind, will you, Son? I sort of think he earned them."

Randy walked over to him. "You know I won't mind. Mr. Sam sure did earn them. And Pa, getting down to the grizzly oughten to be too hard. We can—" He broke off.

"What's the matter?" Jed asked sharply.

Wordlessly the boy pointed. Jed swung around. A hundred feet down the trail a huge sow grizzly came ambling out of the timber, two fat cubs cavorting at her heels. They crossed the trail and vanished into the trees.

Father and son turned and looked at each other. Jed shoved back his Stetson and felt of the blood-caked kerchief binding his forehead.

"There's always another bear to take over when one disappears," he said ruefully. "Well, Randy, I reckon that's the life of a cattleman in Wyoming."

ABOUT THE AUTHORS

GUS TAVO is the pseudonym for Martha and Gustave Ivan of Kilgore, Texas.

Mr. Ivan was born in Budapest. After he came to America he worked mostly as a mural painter, and consequently traveled extensively through the country. Eventually he became an art professor at Kilgore College, where he met and married the chairman of the English Department. He is now retired and devotes his time to the painting of western and wildlife subjects. Mrs. Ivan is, at present, the Director of Guidance and Counseling at Kilgore College.

Mr. and Mrs. Ivan spend most of their summers in northern New Mexico.

A NOTE ON THE TYPE

The text of this book has been set on the Linotype in Baskerville, a recutting of a type face originally designed by John Baskerville (1706-1775). Baskerville, who was a writing master in Birmingham, England, began experimenting about 1750 with type design and punch cutting. His first book, set throughout in his new types, was a Virgil in royal quarto, published in 1757. This was followed by his famous editions of Milton, the Bible, the Book of Common Prayer, and several Latin classic authors. His types, which are distinctive and elegant in design, were a forerunner of what we know today as the "modern" group of type faces.

After his death, Baskerville's widow sold all his punches and matrices to the Société Philosophique, Littéraire et Typographique (totally embodied in the person of Beaumarchais, author of *The Barber of Seville* and *The Marriage of Figaro*), which used some of the types to print the seventy-volume edition, at Kehl, of Voltaire's works. After a checkered career in France, where they dropped out of sight for some years, the punches and matrices finally came into the possession of the distinguished Paris type founders, Deberney & Peignot, who, in singularly generous fashion, presented them to the Cambridge University Press in 1953.

The book was composed, printed, and bound by The Haddon Craftsmen, Scranton, Pa. Paper manufactured by S. D. Warren Co., Boston, Mass. Typography and binding design by Betty Crumley.